DEAD ROOTS, WILTING FLOWER

a novel by
Anthony D. Carr

*Walter,
Somethin*

ACARRA Publishing

ACARRA Publishing
23644 Plum Valley Drive
Crete, Il 60417

Copyright © 2003 by Anthony D. Carr

All rights reserved. No part of this book may be reproduced in any form without the prior written permission, excepting brief quotations in connection with reviews written specifically for inclusion in magazines or newspapers.

This novel is a work of fiction. Names, characters, places, and incidents are either the product of the author's imagination or are used fictitiously. Any resemblance to actual events or locales or persons, living or dead, is entirely coincidental.

Manufactured in the United States of America

Library of Congress Cataloging-in-Publication Data is available

ISBN 0-970-77611-X

*This volume is dedicated
to one who was taken
away much too soon -
God Speed
Miyuki*

Prologue

Turning eighteen was the biggest event in O'ne Gold's life. The attorneys were bringing over the papers to transfer control of her trust. The ringing doorbell signified to her that the long wait for the bulk of her trust to be released to her control was over. No longer would those who had over the years, asserted their will over her be able to continue to do so.

O'ne answered the door at what once was her father's house. She was met by what remained of a black woman. The woman at the door, over the years, had given her all in the service of others and was now, in her twilight, frail and empty looking. Yes, over the years Attorney Ireane Holt had served her community well.

"Hello. Is O'ne Gold in?" The hollow form inquired through the front entrance's iron security door.

Noticing the effect that the winter wind was having on the elderly woman, O'ne opened the door without hesitation.

"Won't you please come in," O'ne offered in a very, innocent proper voice that told of the years of private education that she had endured.

As she entered the home, Attorney Holt took the time to look O'ne up and down and admire the effect that time, good schools, and money had had on her.

"Thank you. I take it that you're Ms. Gold?" Attorney Holt asked.

"Yes," O'ne responded in a reserved but excited voice. "You must be here concerning my trust?"

"Yes, in a way. My name is Ireane Holt. I am a partner in the firm of Dickerson, Carter, Holt and Finch. At one time, I was your father's attorney and I have been entrusted with a task."

The senior woman's internal reflection into the distant past caused the thin, almost transparent hair that ran from the base of her neck down her back to stand on end.

O'ne was just a bit confused by the woman and was now hoping that she hadn't made the mistake of inviting the unknown into her home. Already having opened the door to this exchange, O'ne decided to adhere to her manners.

"Please sit down, Ms. Holt. Can I take your coat?"

"Thank you, but I think that I will keep it on for a while. The cold out there has had its way with me and I don't know if I will ever get warm."

Dead Roots Wilting Flower

"Do you need something to warm you up? What about some tea?"

"That would be nice if it wouldn't be too much trouble," Attorney Holt responded.

Leaving the room, O'ne was surprised at how comfortable she had become with this woman in the last thirty seconds or so. It was as if they already knew each other. Thinking further, she concluded that it had to be the woman's age and style.

The woman's black full-length mink coat, black-on-black tailored dress suit, and Evon Picone dress boots comprised the sort of outfit that she herself would wear. Everything was in place, until it came to an old and tattered oversized briefcase that the woman carried into the house and that now rested at her feet.

O'ne returned with a tray containing two oversized mugs, sliced lemon, several designer tea bags, and a crystal bowl filled with sugar.

"It will be just a few more minutes for the water to boil," O'ne told the woman, giving her a reassuring smile. "While we're waiting, tell me what brought you to see me?" O'ne's anticipation showed all over her face.

Before the request was fully out of her mouth, O'ne noticed that the older woman's legs were shaking. The movements were not like the shivering that comes from being cold. The movements had a timing to them, which was calming to O'ne's eyes.

Attorney Holt noticed O'ne's stare and instead of trying to control her shaking responded, "It's the only thing that calms me and keeps the visions at bay."

"What kind of visions?" O'ne asked, her interest being piqued.

"I think they surround unfinished business. Maybe they will stop after today," Attorney Holt wished as she spoke.

"I see things too." O'ne surprising herself, had spontaneously entrusted this woman with a revelation that no one else knew about.

When O'ne was young, she thought everyone had visions. As she grew older, she discovered that she was the only one she knew who had them. As time went on, she refrained from speaking about them for fear that she would be thought of as strange.

"Up until now I thought that I was the only one them. I mean I've never met anyone who — you know what I mean," O'ne continued, feeling her way through a subject that was sensitive for her.

"Yes, O'ne, I know what you mean," Attorney Holt consoled, as much with her eyes as with the words that came from her mouth.

"I don't remember my daddy or, for that matter, my mama either. My mother's side of the family talks about my dad like he was the second coming of the devil."

"Hmm," was the only sound that came from the woman who was now watching the young girl very closely, trying to judge her sincerity.

O'ne cautiously continued: "When I feel him — I mean think of him, he warms me all over, and I just know that he was a good person."

O'ne's underdeveloped powers of observation did not reveal to her that Attorney Holt's shaking had intensified when she had begun to speak of her father.

"Yes, he was a good man and he loved and fought for you dearly. You know, things are not always how they seem," Attorney Holt said, more by way of relishing in her memories than to inform O'ne.

"I better get that tea kettle," O'ne said and left the room to retrieve it.

The teakettle had been whistling for quite a bit as the two women talked in the living room. Reaching the stove, O'ne picked up the kettle with a potholder and waved it back and forth to make sure that there was enough water to fill the two mugs.

O'ne returned to the room and began to pour the boiling liquid into the mugs. Attorney Holt had already taken the time to place an Earl Grey tea bag in her mug, along with some sugar and lemon.

A comfortable silence filled the room as the two women concentrated on getting their tea just the right strength. Attorney Holt took a few sips of the tea and felt warmed and slightly more at ease. The older woman knew that it was time to get to the task at hand.

"O'ne, as I said earlier, I was your father's attorney. I know that you are aware of the major trust fund that is due to convert to your control now that you have come of age."

O'ne couldn't help the toothy smile that overtook her face at the mention of her trust fund. It's not every day that a girl gains control of a fund worth three-quarters of a million dollars.

Attorney Holt continued: "I'm not here about your money. I have been entrusted with a different obligation."

As O'ne heard the words, the smile began to drain from her face, and it was replaced by a look of puzzlement. As the younger woman's face was making this transformation, the older woman reached into her time-weathered briefcase and pulled out an oversized goldenrod envelope.

From the envelope she withdrew a three-inch-thick parcel and a small business envelope. Attorney Holt's entire body was shaking as she handed the fifteen-year old documents over to the young woman.

No words were required. From directions that had been haunting her for years, O'ne knew to open the small envelope first. After opening it, she read the letter aloud.

10/25/03

Dearest O'ne,
I know that you don't remember me but I was one of your daddy's friends. I like to think that your father and I were more than that, but there wasn't time for anything more. Anyway, I feel your daddy calling me now, so I know that I don't have much time. Please read the manuscript. I wrote the words just as they came to me. He wanted you to know, and of course, I wanted you to know and remember. The manuscript will help you just in case your memories are not quite as clear as mine.

Your daddy's friend,

Kayla

"I've waited over fifteen years to know what was in that package. Can you, I mean if it is not too much trouble, can you read a little of the manuscript while I'm still here?" Attorney Holt asked.

"Of course," O'ne replied, really wanting the woman to stay at least until she opened the package and found out what she was in for.

O'ne tore open the parcel and began to read for herself and for Attorney Holt.

Chapter 1

The joy that one would expect to accompany a move to a new city, a new job, and a new condo evaded Kayla Wright. Most of the people, looking from the outside of Kayla's life rather than from the inside, assume, that she had it made.

It was true that Kayla's eight years of higher education were paying off with many comforts. However, a nice car, a home full of things, nice clothes, and more money than she could spend were not enough to fill the voids that her life and experiences had placed upon her.

The voids in her life gave her a feeling of endless tumbling. The tumbling sensation was sometimes fast and out of control, but usually it was slow. Slow, but there all the same.

Tonight, sleep avoided her for the second night in a row. "How can this be happening to me again?" Kayla wondered quietly to herself while her left hand smoothed the cream-colored bed sheet that she lay upon.

Kayla was hoping that her sleepless nights were just the result of her inner self-longing for what was normal to her: the sounds of New York, the smells of New York. In a moment of weakness, she allowed herself to wonder if James Anderson of New York was what she really needed?

Lying on the bed, Kayla shifted onto her back and stared at the blank screen that her bedroom's flat cream ceiling provided. James came to her in a most natural way. Comforted by the thin sheet wrapped around her, a warm feeling overcame Kayla. It was the same feeling that she often felt in her insides when James would wrap her neatly into him on an already warm night.

Wanting to feel what she was feeling, Kayla allowed herself to flow deeper into her thoughts. About now, James' body would be forming itself perfectly around her emotional and physical needs. As she felt his comfort rising, she began enjoying the warmth of his body and his cooling warm breath on the back of her neck.

As they lay there, the only empty space between their two bodies was that required to accommodate James' thick vanilla-colored dick. No words were required. When two bodies are meant to be one, clearly no words are required. "It was always good with James," Kayla thought to herself as she began to remember how it all started.

"I can't believe that I asked him out," she laughed to herself.

Dead Roots Wilting Flower

For over a year, on different teams, they had worked closely on several high-profile New York City/Kings County projects. Kayla had come onto the city team about five years earlier. The work was focussed on city planning for revitalization efforts in the city's Harlem area. James was her county counterpart.

James' presence exhibited an arrogance that said, "My shit doesn't stink." Kayla thought, "Let me be the first to tell you that it does — both literally and figuratively." However, he just did it for me, she reminisced.

James had measurements of 36-72-100s and that suited her just fine. At thirty-six, she figured that he was old enough to have spent some of that wildness that most black men need to release. Thinking back, she realized that she had never contemplated that a man who looked as good as he did might not want to let go of the playboy trapped inside of him.

This man has eyes to die for she mused. Just your basic dark-brown, but they have a glisten to them when he speaks that transforms everything he says into something sexy. Oh, what a chill she got just thinking about them. Those sexy brown eyes were encased in oval sockets lined with long black lashes that gave the illusion that eye liner and mascara had been applied to them.

Her second criterion, a good looking body, was met at a glance. James was well over the standard seventy-two inches that she required — about six foot six. His body was not bulky as are some men's who let themselves go after thirty. He was clearly built for speed, and a woman could lose herself fast with this type of man.

The icing on the cake was his salary: one hundred sixteen thousand dollars a year. A known fact because a county employee's salary is a matter of public record.

Kayla ventured deeper into her thoughts, and it was like she was back in time with James. She had kept her desires for this man a secret from him and almost from herself until one day, on impulse, it hit her. Even today, she still wasn't sure what had attracted her so compellingly. Was it his French vanilla toned skin or was it the way his tightly locked curls of jet-black created a mane that perfectly contrasted with his skin.

No, right now at this moment, she felt sure that it was his facial hair — all of it. From his thick, black eyebrows to his finely trimmed heavy mustache, there was nothing out of place. Even the slight smile that crossed his full lips when he had heard her invitation to dinner didn't look out of place. Hey, she thought, was he reading my mind? If he was, he was right on target — I was gone. My insides were rambling like a compact car, not built for speed, being driven way too fast.

The sound of a nighttime fire engine whistled past her building causing a slight, hardly noticeable trembling of its windows and walls. The rumbling of the building was just enough to waken Kayla from her trance-like state. Usually, she did not have these deep trances, which seemed like out-of-body experiences, about things in her recent past. Come to think of it, she hadn't had one at all since she had been seeing James.

Generally, her uncontrollable reflections into the past were about things that she had no personal knowledge of.

Dead Roots Wilting Flower

The intensity of her memories and feelings many times was overwhelming. When the feelings came, they were both physical and mental and sapped all of her strength. It was almost as if she were actually living in the past.

"I don't miss that bastard," Kayla said just loud enough to have been actually talking to someone if they had been in her bedroom.

Catching herself slipping back to that trance-like place again, Kayla raised herself out of bed and began to pace the spacious room. While walking and going nowhere, she made mental notes of the things that she had accomplished in the past week and the things she wanted to do to make her new bedroom the sanctuary that she needed it to be. She envisioned a room filled with pastel colors, flowers, and plants. A room that could make a day's stresses pale in comparison.

While she was giving the room the once over, she noticed the slightest of scratches on the rear leg of one of her night stands. The burlwood on the Georgio furniture held a special place in her heart. The furniture was the first big-ticket item she had ever purchased. It was her self-reward for the completion of her joint Juris Doctor - MBA degree at Columbia University. The degree was a turning point in her life, but it had not changed her. She remained down to earth about most things. However, it was clear that her bedroom set was not one of them.

Kayla's humble beginnings had taught her that to excel in this man's world, her work ethic needed to be strong and most likely her sacrifices would be many. Having had to face the prospect of robbing Peter to pay Paul on a daily basis to stay in school, she now was much more appreciative of this time of fruitful bearing.

The purchase of her bedroom set — which she had coveted from her first year at Columbia — gave her a feeling of accomplishment like nothing else that she had done since.

Back then, on the days when work, school, people — just life as a whole — seemed unbearable, Kayla would stop into Vindetties' furniture store just to admire the bedroom set. Looking at the set, she could escape from the day's realities, if only for a short period of time, and push herself somewhere else, somewhere in her own future. Kayla's fantasy included a solid career, a good man, two point five children.... But all of that, including the bedroom set, was just a dream at the time, an escape from the realities of the day.

It wasn't as if she could not have signed her name and at 21 percent owned at least a small part of her dream. But to do so would make the bedroom set a part of the problem and not the solution that it is providing. In many ways the set represented a place to put her troubles. It was a way to escape so that she could concentrate on her studies and life wouldn't become overwhelming.

"I'm going to get that bedroom set," Kayla would mumble to herself, leaving the comfort of the store and beginning her walk through the downtown district with no clear destination in mind. While walking, she would notice the appearance of other people. Most, in some form or fashion, were trying to show their measure of success.

Many of the people on their way to work affected a look that said the weight of the world was being dragged behind them. Their current state of mind would not allow them to have a meaningful exchange with the world around them. They didn't see any difference between the career bum that asked for money on the same corner every day and the tourist who approached them to ask for directions. Both the bum and the tourist were given equally unapproachable looks by the hard-bitten commuter.

From time to time, someone would appear to Kayla to stand out from the crowd. They stood out in a way that their very aura — as communicated by their stride, the look on their face, their overall nonverbal manner — said that they were ready to take on the world.

The beat of the drum, playing silently behind them, transmitted a feeling that they were in charge of their destiny. Not a reckless feeling, but one that said, "Come on world; bring it on."

Continuing her walk from the furniture store, Kayla noticed a rather short, mousey man who had on a perfectly fitting custom-made suit. Everything about the man's attire was perfection. He was sporting French cuffs, with about a quarter-inch of his shirt sleeve showing below the brilliant pin striping of his suit jacket sleeve.

The suit was adorned with a power tie and a tight knot. The tightness of the knot did not seem to restrict his airway or look uncomfortable. This man was quite comfortable. Even with all the power that the tie clearly had, it was still understated and held in place perfectly by a practical tie pin.

Every stride that this man took was taken with his head held up, eyes engaging those that he passed as if he were saying good morning with his eyes to each and every person he passed. Yes, everything was just as you would expect until you got to this man's feet.

To finish his look, this man has chosen a pair of Nike blue and white basketball shoes. The shoes, while color coordinated with the rest of his attire — clearly complementary — seemed funny with the rest of his business clothes. This man was outside the norm. However, the confidence pouring from him made the look work without question.

Kayla made a mental note of this experience, which included her saying to herself very boastfully under her breath, "When I get there, I want that." "That" did not need to be defined. It was enough just to say "that."

ʒ ʒ ʒ

Kayla picked up her day runner and placed an entry to remind her in the morning to phone the moving company and place a claim for the small scratch on the night stand. Since the movers were bonded, she had no doubt that they would make amends for the scratch.

Setting her day runner down on the night stand, she slowly inspected the scratch feeling its depth by running her index finger over it. The feel of the wood almost brought her back into a trance-like state again. She quickly raised from her bending position and headed toward the kitchen to get herself a drink.

Kayla's move from New York City to Chicago had been decided and done over a two-week period. Fast? No, not fast enough. She knew that for her New York was used up and no longer an option. She made up her mind quickly to accept a job that at best could be looked at as a lateral move to Chicago city government.

Dead Roots Wilting Flower

The relocation company found the townhouse in Dearborn Park II. She had only taken a virtual tour of it on the Internet before she wired the realtor the earnest money deposit to secure the home. A week later she arrived in the Windy City on the wings of an American Airlines 757.

She hired a good moving company to move her things from the East Coast to Chicago. The last two weeks had been spent trying to make the townhouse feel like home.

Being used to the privacy of a high-rise building, Kayla gave no thought to walking through her courtyard building dressed in shear nightwear as she headed to the kitchen to find relief. Arriving at her destination, she opened both doors of the side-by-side refrigerator/freezer at the same time and searched for something fulfilling.

The cold air from the ice box gave Kayla a sudden chill over her dark skin. The cool caress of the frosty air caused goose bumps to form on her arms and upper body. The cold air also had the effect of causing her small, upright breasts to become a little tighter.

She searched inside the fridge for something that would ease her longing. Under the duress of the cold air, she quickly chose a lime Le Croix water, retreated from the refrigerator, and made her way into the living room.

Kayla opened the water, took a small sip of it, and took the time to enjoy the taste of the carbonated beverage. As always, the water tickled her palate and caused a slight burn in the back of her mouth.

On her way back to her bedroom, Kayla stopped at the living room's oversized picture window. Looking through the window and into the night, it took a few seconds for her eyes to become adjusted to the relatively bright light streaming into the room from the lights in the courtyard.

A sudden flickering of light through the window caused something to happen within her and without any warning she was back in New York, back in James' arms, lost under the light flowing into her Manhattan high-rise apartment.

"You feel so good baby," James said with his hands. Hands that cupped her butt while he pressed his body almost through hers.

"James, I love the way you hold me," Kayla said with her eyes as she looked up at his face, fully realizing how lucky she was. Her dreams were coming true. She had in her arms the man of her dreams, and for the first time in the longest while the visions of the past were not haunting her. She just knew that in the next few months James was sure to make her complete. In her mind, they were moving toward marriage.

"I want you," James continued talking softly to Kayla with his hands. His hands now covered both of her breasts in a way that still left his thumbs free to lightly caress her nipples through the fabric of her silk pink blouse and shear black bra. As if this weren't enough to get things started, his hips were grinding the length of his sex onto her inner thigh, making her cat burn with anticipation.

"Suu Oh," Kayla's mind moaned just as the bottle of Le Croix hit the hardwood floor splashing ice cold water over her bare feet and ankles.

"Shit, that's cold!" Kayla screamed to no one. The cold, wet awakening brought to the forefront of her mind what the real problem was, the reason why sleep was

Dead Roots Wilting Flower

avoiding her. She had thought that since she was able to control her tears and her heart was only hurting a little that she would be able to put James behind her. But even being halfway across the country from him didn't stop her mind from drifting to what once had been her comfort.

"Damn, damn, damn, I'm not over him yet, am I?" Kayla asked herself as her hand innocently fell from its job of comforting her breast.

Coming the rest of the way out of her reverie, she bent at the waist to pick up the fallen bottle, exposing the bottom of her buttocks. She also noticed that the straps of her gown were off her shoulders and the shear fabric had slid down well past her breasts. The gown, designed for beauty and not for coverage, was already revealing enough. Instinctively, she felt that this was bad and that somebody's eyes must be on her. She quickly folded her arms over her exposure. It was not hard for her to cover up her small breasts. However, still exposed were the feelings of inadequacy that were the natural byproduct of another failed relationship.

Chapter 2

There was nothing good about the swing shift at UPS. The work was hard and the hours cut into the heart of the day, the time when most social interaction took place. Working there meant the loss of hours and days of interaction with people. Time that could never be regained.

Routinely, after work, Albert Gold spent time winding down in his living room, listening to his collection of jazz recordings. A recent purchase of a Sony 300 disc changer allowed him to mostly point, click, and be immersed in sound. Sounds that worked to clear his mind and put him in the best of spirits should be expected after putting in long hours at work.

A recent death had left no woman on Al's agenda. In his effort to endure his current state, he had found that there was only so much music could do. Music could never take the place of the emotional excitement of a loving woman. The worst part of it all was that there was no one to share his love of music.

It was hard for his casual friends to understand that his passion for music extended far beyond the mainstream material that could be heard seven days a week, twenty-four hours a day on Chicago's light jazz station WNUA. His tastes went to Bird, Monk, Bassie, and the like. Most of the commercial recordings that many people liked he could do without.

Al bore a striking resemblance to Samuel L. Jackson. However, at five foot, nine inches he lacked his height. Paper-bag brown in color, most would think him an average looking man with charisma. Al's fitness stood out even when he was fully dressed. His well-defined chest and chiseled butt made many members of both sexes wonder how he would feel in bed.

A black man working, there was really no reason for Al to be alone. However, over the last six months, he had been consumed by grief and the intense court battle that ensued over the custody of his daughter O'ne. The intensity of the case has drained him to the point of not having the energy to do everyday things.

Al knew that his daily pattern was becoming too routine. Workout, work, jazz, sleep; workout, work, jazz, sleep. Just at the right time, two days ago, while house sitting for a good friend, there was a wrinkle added to his routine. It was nameless, yet graceful. To date, it was only a form in the night — a shadow that darted past him and kept him from knowing more about it. Back and forth it went two or three, sometimes four times in the

Dead Roots Wilting Flower

night or early morning hours. Al decided to keep a lookout.

The form had never appeared at the same time over the last two days, but when it did, it was worth every moment of the wait. A wait that included very little thought, thanks to the purity of the music; the purity of the water glass full of Martel XO on the rocks — the rocks being formed from a triple filtering water purification system that ensured crystal clear ice cubes; dreams of a day when his daughter would come to live with him; and, of course today, dreams of the pure form from across the courtyard that he hoped would grace him again.

Al thought to himself, "How could someone nameless and with an unknown personality affect me so?"

He came up with the unreasonable answer that somehow, from the moment he first saw her, she had revealed her essence to him.

"There she is," Al spoke out loud to himself, almost unable to control his excitement.

"Oh, little pretty one," slipped from Al's mouth as he noticed how her granite-colored skin contrasted perfectly with the deep red rose color of her almost too short nightgown. The slight flair at the bottom of the gown shifted from side to side as she walked. The shifting was moving perfectly to the beat of Miles Davis' "All Blues" that was playing at a low level in the background.

The music was playing at just the right sound level so that his sense of hearing would not interfere with his sense of sight, which was of such importance to him right now. In Al's eyes, it was a perfect sight.

The shifting continued as she slowly walked past her window. In the background of her apartment was the glare from a soft nightlight, providing just enough illumination to define her body. Al could see that she was a very dark woman with equally dark shoulder length hair. Straining his eyesight, he could make out, from the shadows, her high cheek bones and the regalness of her walk. The little that he saw made him think of a true Black American Princess.

It had been by accident that he first saw her two nights ago when he had glanced up from reading the inside matter of a new CD that he had purchased earlier that day. He clung to his normal mode of winding down after work even though it wasn't his own home.

His first glimpse of her happened so quickly. From his vantage point, it looked like she was coming directly at him. With no notice, she turned. If not for the two picture windows and the courtyard that separated them, he would have reached out and taken her into his arms.

As it was, his mind did reach out to her with everything that was in him. His mind did not come back empty; it came back filled with wonder and questions. The window consumed his attention. The questions he had about this form rendered his mind and — like never before — his heart wide open.

Before he could completely regain himself, the form appeared again. This time he was able to see her full profile. It looked as though she were actually trying to talk to him through her body language.

"Al, I'm so unhappy during these night-time hours," her wordless actions seemed to say.

It was not lost on Al that even in her state of unhappiness she still showed a type of grace that he had not seen in any of the women that he had dated in the

Dead Roots Wilting Flower

past. It was the grace that was missing from the life of this working-class man. This image possessed an inner glow that showed the world that all was not lost.

As quick as she came into view she was gone. Al sat back in the soft leather chair satisfied. Satisfied even though he knew that his chances with the woman across the courtyard were slim to none. Nevertheless, the three brief encounters with the nameless woman had stirred something inside of him. He knew that sleep would be good that morning.

The following workday went by like clockwork. There was a little something extra in his step. The unknown woman had indeed given him something to look forward to. Never mind that he woke up that morning with a full erection and no one there to provide relief.

While taking his shower, Al used his five girlfriends, who were always at his disposal, to calm himself down. Thinking thoughts of a granite-colored woman, it didn't take long for shots of semen to soil his hand. What little relief that provided took effect. As the last bit of fluid escaped and his throbbing eased, Al grabbed the soap and began to cleanse himself and cleanse the guilt of the five girlfriends from his mind.

That afternoon at work, one of his co-workers, Tracie Brown, must have sensed his need. As she often did, she put the hard press on him. Knowing Tracie as he did, her invitation to come over after the work shift was clearly an inducement to a long night of sex.

Tracie, at five foot-ten-inches tall, was all of 143 pounds. Her frame was a body by Fisher and a face like a rug-rat. Many men admired Tracie's rock-hard body, a body that stimulated men and allowed them to over look over her stringy hair and plain, chocolate-colored acne covered face. Her package, in the past, had led to mostly one-night stands. Those one-night stands were no longer fulfilling for her so, at this point in her life, Tracie wanted much more.

Al had been there before with Tracie and knew that she had some skills.

"Can I take a rain check on that one, Tracie?" Was Al's firm reply.

Al did need the relief, but he did not want it at the expense of being an interloper during his house-sitting that night.

"Are you sure? I can smell a man in heat. You need me tonight — don't you?"

Tracie didn't know the half of it. Al, after a brief moment of weakness, arched his back, and rose to his full height, and replied to Tracie, "You know that you are crazy, girl. Give me that rain check and maybe one day you just might get a run for your money."

Wanting to make her point ever so clear, Tracie walked behind the counter where Al was sorting delivery slips and reached out and took him in her hand.

"You see, you do need me. He's ready for me right now," she said, giving his need a little tug with a skilled hand. "I can almost taste him in my mouth right now," she teased in a seductive tone.

Embarrassed, Al took an instinctive step backward and loosened himself from her light grasp. After moving away, no words were needed. Both of them knew it was not going to happen that night. Al drove the point home with a curt response of, "Not tonight. OK, Tracie?"

Al did not allow himself the luxury of thinking about what he knew would not happen that night. His thoughts were on finishing his shift and getting to his house-sitting duties. Tracie's thoughts for the rest of the shift stayed fixated on Al's zipper and what she wanted.

ʓ ʓ ʓ

At the house, just a bit past 2:00 am, Al was just about to call it a night and hit the shower to wash his current thoughts from his mind when she appeared in his view. It was a quick sighting. He saw her for just the amount of time that it took her to glide across the room.

His breath came hard at the sight of her.

"Oh God, there she is again, right up at the window. Does she see me?" were his thoughts as he remained motionless in his friend's easy chair.

The lack of back lighting in the apartment coupled with his black body and dark clothes blended him into the background of the interior of the townhouse.

For the first time Al was able to see the full contours of her face. The image confirmed her dark shoulder-length hair, high cheek bones and full lips. She was striking, but familiar. There was a sharp contrast between her physical looks and what her eyes showed. Her eyes revealed sadness; and the sadness communicated to Al as if he had spoken to her for hours.

Al read her body language and what it revealed about her, and he felt her pain. Like magic, while she was revealing and he was reading, something happened deep inside of him.

A feeling came over him from head to toe: For the first time in his life he knew how someone else really felt deep inside of themselves. Stripped away from this exchange were the usual layers of protective covering that most keep around them to protect them from the outside world. There in the assumed privacy of her home, Kayla's guard was down and Al saw all.

Al's heart was touched by what he saw. As if in time with the beating of his heart, the nameless form from across the courtyard allowed the straps of her gown to fall from her ebony shoulders unmasking her outermost self to him. Still reading her actions as only he could, Al interpreted her movements to say, "No one could love me if they saw all of me."

Al breathed in deeply at the sight of this woman that he felt so connected to. Within himself he knew that she was wrong about herself. Then, as quickly as it began, it was over. She quickly jerked as if being splashed with cold water and in an instant covered herself and disappeared from view. She was gone and all of the unknown places within him that were just a moment ago fulfilled were now completely drained.

Chapter 3

Kayla's mind drifted off again as soon as she returned to bed. With the newness of her surroundings, her bed was the only place in Chicago that really felt safe and comfortable to her. It didn't take long for her to become entranced in deep thought.

Her current thoughts flowed so vividly that it was as if she had never stopped thinking about James. These thoughts were not like the fulfilling thoughts that were with her just minutes earlier. The memories of her last conversation with James were disturbing to her. Kayla was thinking of their last meeting in New York when she had met James at their favorite eatery at his request. Deep into her trance-like sleep, she began to relive her past.

♋ ♋ ♋

Kayla was awakened early by the annoying ringing of a phone that was purposely placed on the other side of the room from her bed. With the phone placed far away, there was no chance that her normal mode of answering the phone while half asleep and forgetting the conversation as she fell back into slumber would occur.

Trudging her way across the room and trying to keep her eyes closed, she could not fathom anyone calling her this early in the morning with good news. After answering the phone, she was abruptly shaken out of her sleepwalking state by an air of urgency in James' voice.

From his voice, she knew that something important was on his mind. In all the years that she had known this man, there had never been a time when he had seemed unnerved until now.

Kayla spent the morning not knowing what was really on James' mind. All he had offered during his early morning phone call was that they needed to sit down and talk as soon as possible. Enduring a morning of not knowing what was going on with him made time creep by. She watched the clock in her office constantly until it was time for her to leave and meet him.

"Hey, Kayla, sit down."

"Look James, trying to calm me down is just putting me more on edge. I've been worried about what's wrong with you since you called this morning. Come on, just tell me what's going on!" In the back of her mind, she was filled

Dead Roots Wilting Flower

with anticipation, thinking that this might be the day that he would pop the big question.

"It's really nothing — I just think that you have the wrong impression about us and about me, that's all." His statement was huffed out of his lungs and flowed through his mouth and across his lips as casually as you would say good morning to someone that you barely knew.

Noticing that James' facial expression didn't change as he tore into her heart unsettled her enough to speak words of passion.

"Wrong impression?" she queried while her heart was beginning to break.

There was a long pause after the question during which Kayla repeated back to herself James' hurtful words. She had to do this to be sure of what she had just heard.

Now, fully comprehending, she continued.

"What kind of impression was I supposed to be getting during these last few months?" she questioned.

"Calm down, girl, you're getting a bit too loud," he requested, still wearing the same "this is no big deal" look on his face as he quickly looked around the room.

It was becoming clear to her that he was more concerned with what the people in the restaurant were thinking than how his words were affecting her.

"OK, let me see; this past week, Monday, you were at my house. Tuesday, you were at my house. Wednesday, Thursday, Friday, Saturday, and Sunday the same thing. Hell, on most of those days, I damn near had to kick you out of my bed. How in earth's creation could I get the wrong impression unless you gave it to me?"

Seconds went past without an answer to her question. As the building seconds of time quietly crept by and added up, Kayla became more and more agitated. Catching herself in the process of putting her clown uniform on right there in a public place, she slowly and quietly counted to herself, "One, two, three," under her breath, in an effort to calm herself. The three seconds that she counted went by in about an hour.

Now in control, Kayla continued. "We've been very good together James. I don't know what kind of wrong impression I could be getting."

The words were spoken with the sincerity of someone who truly needed to understand. She was in need of gaining something that would make sense of what was unthinkable just a few minutes ago.

It must have been her new found calmness that gave James the courage to begin to speak once more.

"Baby, the last five months have been great."

The beginnings of a smile showed on the edges of James' lips as he reflected. Getting back to the task at hand, James continued. "Remember when this thing first started I told you that there was someone else from out of town? Now they're coming here and we're going to get together and . . ."

Kayla cut him off. She could not believe that he was trying to give the prize that she had worked so hard for to someone else. In her mind the prize had been won by her and was hers. He was hers and, finally, the last piece of a dream puzzle was supposed to be put in place.

Her mind raced and repeated, "Engaged to someone else!"

She could not believe how in less than five minutes her mental state could be changed one hundred eighty degrees. Gone was the calm of the last five months of happiness. What were they to do now? Act as if they never met? Her old feeling of tumbling was back. She could not get hold of this situation.

Out of control, she continued. "James, you told me not to worry about that relationship! You led me to believe that you had taken care of that. That it was behind you!"

Seeing her attitude change, James returned to his "this is no big deal" nonverbal sitting position and assumed that same calm look. Kayla was now totally out of control and in full effect. Anger had engulfed her.

"What is it, James? Huh?"

With her body movements not under her control, she reached out and pushed James out of his leaning forward, "this is no big deal" position at the table. James quickly returned to his former position as if she had not pushed him and calmly said, "Kayla, please calm down and lower your voice."

"Don't you dare try to tell me what to do!"

James cut her off with a sarcastic reply. "If that's how you want it, then so be it."

As soon as the words were out of his mouth he knew that it was the wrong thing to have said to a woman as upset as Kayla was. It was too late, the words were out of his mouth and there was no way to get them back now.

As one might expect, in milliseconds he was wearing, on his face and lap, two glasses of ice water that once sat quietly on the table. Kayla was standing and seemingly towering over James, who smartly remained steadfast in the deep recesses of his chair.

Still beyond herself, Kayla's voice became loud and she didn't care who might hear her.

"What is it, James, I'm not good enough for you to have a really truthful relationship with? Huh?"

James just sat there looking dumbfounded without saying a word. The look on his face made it clear to everyone, since many onlookers were now engulfed in this confrontation, that he had no clue as to what he had just taken from her.

A thoughtful man would have known that Kayla might never fully recover from the hurt that he had placed on her heart. James had no concept that this kind of hurt could call into question whether another man could ever make his way past the mile-thick concrete that his callus act alone had placed all over Kayla's heart.

James, making no reply, just sat there with a stupid look on his face while Kayla, relatively quiet but still filled with emotion, continued. "Don't you know that I gave you me?"

A tear started to slowly make its way down her cheek.

"The first and the last," Kayla thought to herself as she wiped it away.

Dead Roots Wilting Flower

The feeling that welled up was not new to her. She knew that she could handle it better this time. This time would be different — no heartache, no tears.

"No tears," Kayla repeated to herself as she grabbed her purse and walked out of her past and into her future.

Chapter 4

At the foot of LaSalle Street in downtown Chicago stood the old Freeman Bank Building. Dr. King had made his office there for the past twenty years. The office was actually two offices made into one by way of two common doorways. In 1906 when the building first opened its doors — the same year that Kayla's grandfather, John Lewis, was born — space in a modern, steel-reinforced building was at a premium.

When the Freeman building opened its doors, its La Salle Street address alone was enough to enhance the stature of one's business. That being the case, at the turn of the century, space in the building's thirty-two floors was neatly carved into tiny cubicle-sized offices to accommodate as many businesses as possible. The office sizes do not begin to accommodate the needs and complexities of today's businesses. So most of today's tenants have at least two offices, if not more, at their disposal.

Kayla, patiently waited for Dr. King to finish up with his three o'clock appointment so that she could get on with hers, set for four o'clock. She glanced down at her Ebel watch and became just a little agitated when she noticed that it was already four-fifteen and she was still in the waiting room.

With nothing else to do, sitting here now, Kayla focused on the amenities of the office and became aware that the office was showing its age. The building's weathering gave Kayla a calm that took her mind off the fact that it was well past her appointment time.

"What the hell," Kayla thought to herself. She knew that the burden, which she had fought for years, of being one with the past had oppressed her for all of her thirty-four years of life and most likely was not going away anytime soon.

Her burden was like the effect that asthma has on sufferers. Not being able to fully grasp what the past was saying to her was like experiencing the inability to inhale a full measure of air into one's lungs. Both of the conditions keep the sufferer from living life to the fullest.

Kayla continued to notice the physical state of the office. The modern updating that was done to the office over the years had not changed the office's overall aged feel. Clearly, an updating maybe with a full gut rehabilitation, would bring increased life back to the nearly century-old structure. The northeastern view from the office window revealed a breathtaking view of the downtown skyline and lakefront. Another office facelift would not do justice to the superb view from the office window.

The longer she sat in the office's aged waiting room, the more Kayla began to feel the essence of the past that the building held silently within its walls. Somehow, the office's hardwood trim and aged state symbolically told Kayla that the room could withstand the stresses and strains of the emotional outpours that it had to endure on a daily basis from the many patients who were at their wits end.

Kayla continued to slip away as she heard faintly the sounds of flowing, seeping, and dripping water. To her, it seemed that the water sounds were coming from behind the walls of the room. In her mind, there was a damp, musty smell that was growing in intensity by the second. The intensity of the smell was not overpowering, but a smell of dampness that accompanies an area that has been wet for some time and has not been allowed to air out.

Kayla knew that there was no actual reason for her to feel the way she did or smell the scent she smelled. However, she also knew that it was too late. She tried as hard as she could to fight it. Too late — she was going there again.

ℑ ℑ ℑ

The men who worked the mine named it Lucy. At age twenty-six, John Lewis was a fourteen-year veteran of the Alabama mines and already had four years in with Lucy. Over the last fourteen years, John had worked his way up through the ranks. At twelve, for penny tips, he made his way as a runner. From up top to deep within the mine shaft and sometimes all the way into town, he would run for the men that were hard at work within the mine's bowels. The energy of youth allowed him to push himself to make money doing a job that had no glamour. He was basically a flunky.

Hard work over the years paid off for John. As a loader, gone were the days of demeaning work running for pennies. Those days were replaced with the back-breaking task of placing chunks of black rock, forced off the walls of the mine shaft, into rail cars.

His interests eventually led him to where the men of the blasting crew were clearing the way. Over the years, his eyes watched and his ears listened for the small things that someone in this type of work had to know.

His eyes saw many different men with different skill levels come and go. What he learned from them was that doing the dangerous blasting work was an art form and not a job at all. As the different blasting crew chiefs came and went, John gained knowledge.

He gained the type of knowledge that only can be gained by the humbling oneself in subservience to the twenty or so men who had held the position of blasting chief at the different mines where he had worked over the years. He had seen the good and the bad ones and retained the best each had to offer.

John's knowledge included how to look at the shaft's bracing, the slope of her walls, how much dynamite was required, how deep to set the charge. At some point he transformed from student to connoisseur of the subject of blasting in this environment.

It was clear to John that there was a characteristic common to men who were not cut out for this sensitive job. Most of the unsuccessful ones were well over the top with confidence. It was over-confidence that led blasters to miss something. Nothing big, mind you. However, when blasting in a mine's confined space, where the smallest detail can mean the loss of many lives, missing something, no matter how small, can be the difference between life and death.

In a time when the loss of life was an acceptable risk of the industrial revolution that, errors in judgment that cost many months of work and stopped the production of coal were unacceptable.

John's eyes were trained to look out for the small things, things that might have been overlooked. Today, he was looking more with his ears than his eyes.

"Do you hear that?" John asked big Jim.

Big Jim was the chief in charge of the day's blasting activities deep inside Lucy's number one shaft. Jim was mildly annoyed at John's meddling presence. Jim barely missed a beat overseeing the placement of sticks of dynamite in pre-drilled pilot holes in the far wall of the mine shaft as he dismissed John's inquiry.

"Get away from me boy! Get the hell out of the way," Jim snarled and spat deep purple tobacco-stained spit onto the coal black floor of the mine.

"I think there's a lot of water behind that wall, Jim. We should call the engineers down here before we blast that wall," John stated, overlooking Big Jim's dismissal orders. Standing his ground with Jim, John could feel the entire weight of Jim's presence.

Jim was as black as tar and stood all of six foot, five inches tall. His more than 370 pounds — many of which had settled into his stomach over the years — were a commanding presence that made John feel small— almost like the boy that Jim had called him just seconds earlier. In 1931, out in the small town, deep backwoods areas where most coal mines were located in, one's physical presence and power were respected above one's brain capacity.

"Look boooy," Jim started in on John with a sound of astonishment in his voice and a look of disbelief showing clearly through his yellowish eyes, "I told you to get the hell out of my way! I run this hell hole so far as blasting is concerned! You hear me, boy? I'm the damn king down here and what you think don't mean spit!"

Jim's show, put on to impress those around him, was followed with another stream of tobacco-stained spit that fell less then a half inch from John's worn work boot.

Dead Roots Wilting Flower

Less provocation would have caused many lesser men to turn to violence.

With his piece said and his station in the mine seemingly re-secured, Jim ordered the last two pilot holes drilled just that much deeper. He was determined to show the blasting crew who was really the boss.

"No boy is going to show me up," Jim mumbled to himself keeping his blood pressure driven up and his bloodshot and yellow eyes keenly on John as the younger man left the area.

John, knowing what he knew, took the next few seconds, as he walked away, to ponder his next move. What if he was right? What if he was wrong? At that slice in time, at that very moment, at the age of twenty-six, John was forever changed.

For the first time in his life, John was going to step out of the shadows of humility and act as a man should act when something is going wrong. He decided, almost unconsciously, no to defer to Jim. Right now, he was being driven to try what was right.

The mine was laid out with three shafts that branched out from the main shaft where Jim's crew was getting ready to blast. The other two shafts were lower in elevation than the main shaft and would flood if the main shaft flooded. Quietly, shaft by shaft, foreman by foreman, crew chief by crew chief, worker by worker, John told each mine worker to go topside.

Clearly, John did not have the authority to order the men in the shaft to stop working and impact coal production for the day. Instead, he informed everyone that it was the mine's superintendent, Jeb Daniels', decision. "Daniels wants you guys on high ground while they are blasting in shaft number one," was echoed from man to man throughout the long narrow shafts.

In no time at all, with the opportunity to get a break from their sixteen-hour day and out of the cold, damp air that existed deep within Lucy, the mouth of the mine was overflowing with bodies.

"What the hell is going on here?" Jeb yelled at everyone who would listen. He was agitated that coal production had stopped at one of the area's top producing mines.

Jeb was awarded his position the old fashioned way; his daddy owned the mine. Having never endured what a sixteen-hour work day did to a man, he was always full of hot air and unreasonable requests of the workers. It seemed that his only goal in life was to keep Lucy the area's top producing mine no matter what the cost. After all, there were bragging rights at stake with the superintendents of the other area mines.

"What's wrong, Browner? Why are we clearing these men out of the mine?" Jeb Daniels questioned one of Lucy's foremen.

"That kid John said that you wanted us up here while they blasted in number one," Browner replied, defending his action of removing his men from the mine shaft.

Jeb contorted his face, revealing his disgust, and replied, "You mean that I've got over ninety men sitting on their asses because some kid said so! Get your damn people back to work and bring that boy to me! I'm going to whip the black right off his ass!"

The echoing sound of the charges being set off deep within shaft number one could be heard above the chatter and rustling of the workers making their way back down into the bowls of Lucy. With the far reaches of her being over a mile deep, going in and out of her was no small task.

Big Jim called "all clear" and made his way some forty feet to the blasting site from behind the wall that had shielded the members of the crew from the flying rock that the explosion had caused.

"That little bastard isn't going to tell me how to blast," Jim boasted to himself as he joined the seven other men from the crew surveying the results of their work and assessing the need for additional charges to get the job done good and right.

A pronounced cracking sound within the wall suddenly directed eight sets of eyes onto the surface that was just blasted. The next set of events took place in three seconds flat. The wall, with no notice and right before their eyes, imploded, giving way to the force of water behind it.

The men close to the wall had no time to react and most likely never knew what hit them. Jim never had the opportunity to assess the error of his judgment. The other men met their fate under the weight of stone that crushed them. The remaining essence of their bodies and souls was then washed at lightening speed through the shaft by the raging water that had been released and was quickly filling the mine. In no time, the lower recesses of all three of Lucy's shafts were flooded.

The first shouts of flood were heard while the men were just beginning to make their way down the shaft to return to their work stations. The shouts were coming from deep within.

"FLOOD! FLOOD!" someone called from within. The men at the surface bravely rushed down and pushed into Lucy to the point where the water and the shaft met as one. It was clear that all was lost and that days of pumping water out of the mine lay ahead.

In the confusion that the flood caused, Jeb's request to see John was forgotten. All of Lucy's men were focused on the loss of eight lives and how close most of them had come that day to losing their own.

John was found a little more than an hour later with his head in hands. One of his white co-workers called his name. "John, you're a hero boy. Come on here; we're going to town to do some drinking to you. Damn boy, you saved our asses today!"

"That's OK. I'm not really a hero. I just tried to tell Big Jim, but he wouldn't listen. Thanks anyway," John replied not moving to join the men.

It was mostly the same white group that always gathered to hoist a few after work. A few minutes later,

Dead Roots Wilting Flower

John's usual black group of friends joined him and they all went home.

ʓ ʓ ʓ

Ms. Wright, Doctor King will see you now. Over the years, Kayla had seen many doctors. Each one tried to assess her burdens of the past and provide her with relief.

Unlike the other doctors that Kayla had seen over the years, Dr. King's way was less interactive and leaned more toward letting the patient find her own way. He was a good listener who could move and shape his session with a patient with just a few well-placed, simple questions phrased in just the right way.

More importantly, Dr. King never gave off an air of disbelief, no matter how incredible the events were that a patient would reveal.

On its face, Kayla was seeing Dr. King due to her failed relationship with James. However, there was so much more. After their first meeting, Dr. King ordered and had sent to him a copy of Kayla's New York therapist's file. What he read took him back in time.

Chapter 5

Len Edwards sat lazily on the steps of Chicago's Dusable Museum of African American Art waiting for Kayla. He hadn't heard from her for the better part of a year until she called him and told him that she was in town. After her call, instantly Len began making plans to renew his relationship with Kayla.

They had met almost two years ago while on vacation in Las Vegas with friends. She was the only bright spot for him in an otherwise dreadful trip. While in Vegas he lost a great deal of money and a good friend. Out of nowhere, there was Kayla, and like magic Len experienced an instant love connection.

From the distance Len could see Kayla approaching. To him it seemed that everything around her, the green grass, the slight haze in the air, even the rainbow of colors that the late summer flowers displayed, blended and highlighted her in just the right way. Her walk, the look on her face, how her clothes hung just right on her narrow frame foretold of her confidence in her current surroundings. There was something about nature that brought out Kayla's very best. However, her outward look belied what her true state of mind was.

ʒ ʒ ʒ

Walking across the street and spying Len, Kayla continued to daydream about James while looking deeply at, through, and past Len. When she was almost upon him, her face showed the state of pleasure that her thoughts inspired. She looked like a black granite goddess, and her look was not lost on Len.

"You are so beautiful," slipped out of his mouth and into Kayla's ears.

"Why thank you, Len. It's good to see you, too," Kayla responded, retrieved from her thoughts.

"No, I mean it. I don't know what it is but your face is aglow," Len continued.

Kayla just looked at Len again and smiled. It was coming back. Right now it was clear to her how she related so easily to Len. He was truly a charming man. Considering what she recently had been through, it still surprised her how easy it was for her to step right into the comfort zone that Len provided.

Catching herself, she stopped her thoughts. She knew that now was not the time to go off on a rebound with Len. Forcing herself to be realistic, the more she thought

Dead Roots Wilting Flower

about it, the more she knew that there was something missing between them. However, right about now, exactly what that was evaded her.

Len, on a mission, aggressively sought out a hello hug from Kayla to start their reunion off right. When he hugged her, he felt compelled to try to rekindle something by lingering just a bit longer than a friendship hug should. She knew what he wanted when he ran his middle finger across the small of her back the way that he had when they were a couple.

Kayla stood very still, waiting for that feeling to come over her. It didn't come; her panties were dry. Very dry. Completely dry. The reality of the situation did not disappoint her.

The feeling that she needed to have to tell her that this was the right man was not there. Hey, they had their own issues. Issues that Len most likely could not accept. Her dryness made it clear to her that she did not have to share that part of her past and future with him. The quick exchange between them confirmed to her that, at this point, Len was just a warm friend.

"It sure is good to see you girl."

"Len, you haven't changed a bit," Kayla replied thinking back to when they first met. It wasn't hard for her to drift for a second back to how good it had been then.

"It doesn't seem like a year has passed, Len, does it?"

It was a question that she didn't need an answer to because she knew exactly when she had given him the

...en had faded as James' light began to brighten her ...t had been exactly eleven months and two days ...ey last touched. A girl knows what a girl knows.

"You mean a year since you stopped returning my calls." Len could not help himself — he had to get that one in for his own sanity. The instant that it came out of his mouth, mentally reverted back in time to when he was broken into ten pieces by Kayla. Ten pieces hurts. He remembered the seven long days when there was no word from a love that he had spoken with at least once a day for nine months.

The nine months had freely flowed from a hot vacation romance that was full of promise. Over the nine-month romance, Len had taken full advantage of the moment. He put a large amount of his energy into making things work between him and Kayla.

Cards, flowers, short notes, and of course trips to the Big Apple were all part of his commitment to their budding long-distance relationship. Feeling that he had found the one for him, he was ready to take the next step.

Len took a little time to freshen up his résumé with his latest career accomplishments and place it with two different New York headhunters. Knowing the market for art directors at advertising firms, he also put the word out to the powers that be that he was looking for a change of venue.

With his ground work done and knowing that New York was New York, it wouldn't take long for one of the

Dead Roots Wilting Flower

top firms to come along and pick him up. All at once his life was coming together.

ʒ ʒ ʒ

Kayla knew that most women would find Len a great catch. He was fine, tall, and lanky with lemony skin that showed a little age. He was blessed with a broad, full smile that had a way of brightening his eyes.

He was the only man that she had ever seen actually stop traffic with his looks, Kayla remembered. When his gear was on, women would stop their cars just to see him walk down the street; she continued her trip down memory lane.

Kayla began talking to herself as she remembered. I don't know what it was but my heart just didn't skip in the right way for us. I felt so much pressure from him. It's funny, things started off great between us. It must have been the vacation setting warm weather, days by the pool, nights in his arms, long walks and talks. While we were in Vegas, everything was perfect. After leaving Las Vegas, just like a new toy that has played out, his shine started to fade.

She mused that it was just the lights and sounds of Vegas that had made things so great for them. Looking back now, she knew that it was also the intensity of the death of Len's friend, Dee, that drove them together and allowed her to put everything else out of her mind.

When you are in too deep, it's easy to overlook things. Things like personality traits that, in other circumstances, would tempt you to kick someone to the curb without a second thought.

Len's friend's death put his emotions out front for everyone to see. Being the sensitive girl that she was, she could not put the wealth of emotion generated by Len in the proper perspective. All of Len's emotions were right on his sleeve for her to see; for her to feel; for her to bond with. A girl can get used to having her man need her in that way. After the effects of the death started to wear off and Kayla went back to New York, little by little the intensity of the relationship faded.

With things starting to slow down between them, Len started to push things in an unnatural way. He really wanted there to be an "us," she thought. The more he tried, the more all chances for our relationship faded to black. A blackness that you cannot see, but you can feel its presence around you. A feeling that defies words. The natural flow that sustains a relationship stopped cold. She knew that most women would love to have a Len on their arms, let alone sweating them like they were the last woman on earth, but she needed out in a bad way.

Kayla remembered her brain saying "Stay with Len," but a girl sometimes has to turn her heart on full, her mind off, and go with the flow. At that time, James was clearly the flow. He had the flow that swept Len right out of her. The flow that revealed to her what she was actually settling for.

After kissing James and feeling that hot, wet feeling between her legs — a feeling she hadn't felt in years —

Dead Roots Wilting Flower

She was no longer able to settle. If a girl can remember that feeling when love is fresh and new, then settling for a man that can't give it will never be an option. After not having it for so long, getting that feeling was like getting life back.

☽ ☽ ☽

Len and Kayla walked side by side and sometimes hand and hand through the museum's exhibits that focus on African American history. The museum is a place where one can be engulfed by the rich history of people of color. A place where some of the historical voids, that a public school education routinely creates can be filled in.

After leaving the museum, they caught a cab over to Mellow Yellow in Hyde Park. Mellow Yellow, a trendy eatery that caters to the hip University of Chicago and black urban professional crowd, is a place to be seen in.

After settling into the restaurant, Kayla ordered the roasted chicken with macaroni and cheese and collards as her sides. Len ordered his usual strawberry crepes. They both washed their meal down with vanilla malts.

During the course of the meal they became reacquainted. The magic of their friendship was still there and the effect of the year that they spent apart was dissipating.

During the meal, Len thought that things were going well. Even so, Len understood that there was something different. He saw a big "Do Not Enter" sign that warned of a danger zone. It was a sign that Len was used to seeing but had always read as "Enter at Your Own Risk."

Len, being the risk taker that he was, read the sign as one would read a stop sign that had "Go" printed in big letters. He wanted to go there and take the risk.

Len displayed all of the non-verbal signals of a man who wanted to pick up as if time had stopped and the days, months, and year that they were apart would vanish and what was would be again.

Tumbling very fast, it was hard for Kayla to catch herself. On its face, everything about this date was right. The conversation, the restaurant, even when it seemed that Len knew every black person in Chicago and they all wanted to say hello and be introduced all of it was good. After her New York heartbreak and her quick move to Chicago, just hanging out and being herself was a comfort.

Leaving Mellow Yellow, the couple went on and going to the Green Dolphin on the North Side of the city to socialize and listen to some live jazz. The spot was packed with a Saturday after-dinner crowd, a crowd that wanted to avoid the late night shake-your-groove thing bunch. It was a group of people that wanted top shelf everything. Alcohol and service was paramount on their list, and they didn't mind paying for it.

At the club, everyone, including from the coat check girl, bar staff, and well-dressed, fully blending security staff, made the place stand out as a spot where people of various backgrounds and cultures wanted to be.

Dead Roots Wilting Flower

The crowd, which gathered as much to socialize as to listen to the mostly unrefined local jazz acts that usually played there, was diverse. There were twenty something to forty something aged blacks, whites, Hispanics, and Asians, all clicking together in a show of how good it can be when the races truly get along. They were there to release the week's burdens and embrace all that the night might bring.

"I really like this spot," Kayla said to Len just before her thoughts were again interrupted by someone who wanted to say hello to Len.

"What's up Len?" Al's greeting was loud enough to be heard over the volume of the music blaring in the next room.

"Al! What's going on man? Good to see you. You remember Kayla, don't you?" Len's voice was even louder than Al's.

Al looked into Kayla's eyes and immediately knew them. There was no mistake.

"Um ... yeah... um... from Las Vegas, right?" He replied while realizing just whom it was that he had been looking at from across the courtyard.

"Hi, Al. How ya been?" Kayla replied, fully aware of Al's discomfort at seeing her.

In an effort to renew their friendship she leaned toward him and gave him a friendship hug and a kiss on his cheek. She was surprised at how firm and drawn-out her hug with Al was. Something was exchanged between them as they hugged. It was as if he needed to hug her.

The closeness of their two bodies also revealed to her a familiar and pleasing scent of Burberry cologne.

His composure regained, Al remembered the good and bad times that they had had in Vegas. Now, all smiles, he began, "I didn't know that you and Len still stayed in contact with each other."

When the three of them had met in Vegas about two years earlier, they underwent an intense time together. It was the type of experience that loosely binds people together that may have no other connection. Death has that effect on many people.

Al, remembering the early mornings peering through the window across the courtyard, asked, "So what brings you to town? You live in New York, don't you?"

"I moved here four weeks ago. I guess you can say that I'm now a Chicagoan."

"Oh, no. It takes more than just moving here to get that title. You have a lot of Chicago living to do before you can say that," Al joked.

Al looked into Kayla's eyes beckoning for her to reveal her thoughts to him as she had in the recent past. He wanted to see the eyes that had engulfed him from across the courtyard only a few nights before.

"Well, maybe we can adopt you and make your transition easier," Al suggested while looking at Len to see his reaction. Before a reaction could come, a woman came over and demanded that Len talk to her.

"Let's seal our deal of adoption with a drink," Al suggested to Kayla, putting his arm through hers.

"Fine, but that will be an easy living for me. I'm on the wagon for a while," Kayla said involuntarily placing her hand on her stomach at the reason for her words.

Al looked over at Len and mouthed, "I'll be right back."

Al waited for a reply that never came. Len just turned his head in a look of disgust

At the bar, over the next hour or so, Al and Kayla became reacquainted as friends. It didn't take long for Kayla to notice that Al wanted her full attention and was giving her his. It felt good to have a man act like she was the last woman in the world.

"Guess who," Tracie from Al's job asked, walking up behind Al and placing her fingers over his eyes.

"Tracie, I would know your voice anywhere," Al replied.

It was a voice that any Saturday morning cartoon character would die to have.

Tracie walked around the bar stool and presented herself to Al and Kayla.

"Tracie, I want to introduce you to Kayla. Kayla, this is Tracie."

Tracie, being a little standoffish, looked Kayla up and down.

Kayla, noticing Tracie's look, broke the ice.

"I ain't the one, girl. He's not mine. Do you want him?"

"Naw, girl, I can't even give it away to him. I've been trying, though," Tracie stated showing much attitude.

"Wait a minute. What am I? A piece of meat that you guys think is just a bit too ripe? Well I've never." Al played right along with the women.

The conversation among the three of them stayed light over the next ten minutes or so until the ebb and flow of the room took Al from them and sent him off talking basketball with a group of guys a little way down from where Kayla and Tracie were still talking.

Kayla's meeting Tracie was a godsend. Moving to a new city there are so many things a girl needs to know. Where to shop, where to get a touch-up and fly cut, or just where to get a fresh manicure. The list goes on and on. Besides that, just having another woman to call and talk to without having to dial her mother long distance would be perfect.

Needing Tracie, Kayla latched onto her and hung on as if her life depended on this new-found potential friend.

"Girl, give me your number so that we can finish this conversation," Tracie suggested.

Before the words were out of her mouth, Kayla had reached into her purse and pulled out a newly printed business card with her work information on it.

Handing Tracie the card, she reminded her, "Now I need you to call me on Monday so you can give me the number of your beautician."

Tracie picked up a napkin from the bar, as many men had done to jot down her number in the past, and wrote down her home phone number and handed it to Kayla.

"I know what it's like to be in a new place. Call me anytime about anything you need Kayla."

"OK, Tracie, I'll talk to you."

Tracie gave Kayla a girlfriend hug, the type of hug that is generally reserved for long-term girlfriends.

After Tracie left, Kayla found herself alone at the bar. She quickly found Len, not wanting to be perceived as one of the many women in the room that wanted the company of a strange man.

The rest of the evening flew by, and it wasn't long before Len was at Kayla's door saying goodnight. Len made it clear that he didn't want the night to end. Leaning forward, eyes closed, he waited for the type of kiss that she used to supply at the drop of a hat. He wanted a kiss and a feel of her body to confirm his standing with her.

Kayla's voice woke him from his delusion.

"Um, no. I'm not ready for that and neither are you. You have no idea what is going on with me, and you just assume that we could pick up where things left off."

"I'm sorry, but for me it's like we have never been apart," Len offered in support of his impulsive move for a kiss.

"Good night, Len."

Closing the door behind her, Kayla's thoughts drifted over the day's events and lingered on Al.

"He is a nice guy, isn't he," she said out loud to herself.

Chapter 6

Al was driving south way too fast down the Dan Ryan expressway trying to get home. In the back of his mind he wished that his house-sitting duties had not ended. Disagreeably, his head was clear and unclouded. The five Glen Livets on the rocks that he drank that night at the Green Dolphin, many hours ago, had long since worked their way through his system.

To his dismay, the drinks were having no further effect on him. Scotch on the rocks had become his drink of choice since being introduced to it by a good friend almost two years before. He wanted the drinks to help keep his attitude positive.

Without the help of alcohol, this late night drive would be filled with thoughts about his problems. He was alone since he had declined the advances of his co-worker Tracie. Problems had been affecting his state of mind for some time.

ɔ ɔ ɔ

As Al made his way past 47th Street, his last conversation with Terow, his last girlfriend, began playing in his head as if they were taped on Memorex.

"This just ain't going to work," Al said disapprovingly to Terow as they pulled up to a three-flat brownstone apartment building on 83rd and Ada on the city's Southwest Side.

"Its gotta work! You just don't understand, do you?" Terow asked.

Terow's eyes were glazed over, holding back tears that Al would never know existed, as she spoke.

"Te, what I do know is that with a new baby and being on maternity leave, leaving your mom and dad's house right now is crazy. There's not enough money to go around," Al said excitedly, in a loud but reasoned tone.

"What about you? She's your child, too! Baby this can work," Terow reasoned back, the hope in her eyes and voice still evident.

"Look, Babe, I'm going to help but remember I have other responsibilities that I can't just turn my back on."

What Al didn't disclose was that he already had plans for a new house that didn't include moving into the brownstone with her. His other plans already had him stretched to the limit.

"I'm not asking you to turn your back on anything. I just want the best for us, Al. Can't you see that?" she questioned.

"Girl you know that I'm spread too thin already."

Listening to Al and his excuses as to why they should not move into the brownstone's third-floor apartment, Terow's outward and inner demeanor changed in an instant.

"Well, Al, you don't have to worry about us. Just take me back to the hospital. I think it's time for O'ne's feeding."

All of the positive energy that had been generated between the two of them just seconds before was gone. In the time that it took to blink an eye, Terow and Al became like ships passing in the night. Once so close now they were so very far apart in their thinking, their wants, and their desires.

Riding silently in the passenger seat of Al's car, Terow wondered to herself how it could be that he just did not get it. Wasn't all that she had done for them clear to him? The apartment, the furniture, everything was done. She wasn't asking him for much — just for him to be with them. Everything else would be OK if he could just get it.

A break in time occurred and a connection was broken. The result broken off from the whole, bore no resemblance to its former self. With the break, Terow became a new person with a different set of issues.

Terow had never envisioned herself as a single mother before this very instant. Now, at this slice in time, it became crystal clear to her that Al was not going to be their knight in shining armor. A knight that would make her world and her daughter's world safe from all dangers. Al was just a man who had, in her mind, fallen off his knightly horse and become common.

In her dreams, Terow did not see a common outcome being in her future. Her thoughts demanded that she not fall into the all too common role of loving too hard. She would not, could not, allow herself to continue to love a man who would not be her and her child's knight.

In the next slice of time, that piece of her that had broken off and transformed itself lashed out at the remainder. That piece, not needing to be whole anymore, understood that the remainder was expendable. Terow's sharp tongue dealt the first blow to the remainder with hurtful venom.

"Something bad is going to happen to you," was her simple statement, said in a way that cut to the bone.

"What do you mean?" Al questioned.

"Never mind. You're too stupid to understand anyway," Terow stated, threatening to start cutting into the bone that was now fully exposed.

"What's wrong with you, girl?" Al replied, totally taken aback by the change in Terow's attitude.

Al saw none of her former compassion as he glanced at Terow from his straight forward driving position.

Dead Roots Wilting Flower

"Look, just keep your eyes on the road. You know that you can barely drive as it is," she exclaimed.

After that, the interior of Al's BMW 540IL fell silent and the hum of its German engineering could be heard like a bass drum. Not understanding Terow's sudden change, Al replayed her last comments in his mind and became more and more unsettled. The words "something bad is going to happen to you" were engrained in his mind. The statement was more warning than most received before their adversary took action against them in the South Side streets of Chicago.

Al knew that Terow could reach out and touch (hurt) him if she wanted to. She had the means. Her upbringing and double life as a college student and a major gang enforcer's baby sister gave her all the means she needed.

Looking at her now, with her pageboy haircut lying perfectly on her caramel-candy-colored, slightly-too-big-for-her-face forehead — a look that told of her unique style — one would never guess that she grew up hard and streetwise.

Up until now, Terow's bad girl past never worried Al. In fact, her being able to handle herself was a turn-on for him. With her attitude and the warning, Al knew that he was exposed. Exposed to an unknown that could hurt him. In deep thought, Al just wondered if her warning was for real.

Al's car sped down the road at what seemed like a million miles per hour to him as his mind reentered the present.

"Shit! I missed the damn exit," Al shouted out loud to his thoughts.

The shout quieted the unwanted memories that were continuing to cause his mental state to crash. Over the past three months, Al had gone from a sure-minded person, able to set his sights and get what his sights were set on, to one who could barely muster enough energy to get up in the morning and face the day. Just one day without worry was what he needed.

"Ever since that accident I just haven't been myself. God, what am I going to do," Al asked to the oncoming car lights that shined brightly into his eyes.

Al was slipping back into deep thought again. He bore a heavy burden of guilt. In his mind, it was clear, that his refusal to move in with Terow forced her to take a second job.

"No wonder she fell asleep behind the wheel and got herself killed. She was trying to do too much," Al mumbled to himself, continuing to drive.

"A baby, two jobs, and classes at Chicago State. If I had only known. If I had only known," Al's thoughts continued to beat him up until he pulled into his driveway in Chicago's Beverly Hills neighborhood.

Chapter 7

It was just after Terow's death that Al purchased the 1940s vintage graystone mini-mansion. He knew the history of the house and the accompanying carriage house behind it.

The estate at one time had more than seven acres of rolling grass, gardens, and trees around it. At the time that it was built, the Beverly area was the preferred setting for many the country homes of Chicago's elite.

With changing times, most of the acreage around Al's home had been sold off to developers more than forty years ago. The remaining acre lot was more than enough to complement the home's grand appearance.

Over the years, since his childhood, Al had worked the grounds of the estate. During the harsh Chicago winters, he spent time caring for the home's hardwood floors and Italian tile. The home was as fresh today as it was when it was built in the early forties.

Al had to have the house. It would be a stretch, but if he tightened his belt and took hold of each of his expenses he could pull it off. He would have this house no matter what.

ʒ ʒ ʒ

Growing up as a boy and well into his twenties, Al had had a relationship with his house and its occupant. His first exposure to the house was by way of cutting grass for his math tutor, Ms. Snider. Ms. Snider was a former high school teacher who was nice enough to donate her time to an inner city after-school tutoring program. From the beginning, it was clear to Ms. Snider that Al was different.

When she met him, he was twelve and surprisingly not jaded by the harshness of his inner-city environment. Many of the kids Al's age, in his west Englewood neighborhood, usually had their smiles all but wiped from their faces by the harshness of unchecked city living.

Al never knew his father and to the best of his knowledge his father never knew of him. By the time he hit his preteen years, it was not uncommon for Al to ramble into the night trying to find his mother. She had a habit, and when a monkey was on her back, it was really on her back. Stability came in the form of a grandmother

Dead Roots Wilting Flower

who still thought that it was nineteen forty when it came to using a tree limb as a switch.

In spite of the burned out buildings, boarded up stores, and despair that surrounded Al, a relationship between a twelve-year-old boy and a fifty-eight-year-old Jewish survivor of Germany's World War II concentration camps was formed. What was shared between the unlikely pair was the feeling of having been hated for no other reason than their race.

Greta Snider was just a shadow of her former self. As a young teenager, when she was taken, she was vibrant. She remained vibrant and glowing even after enduring over three months of hell in the camp. They raped her and left behind a seed that, coupled with miscarriage, would forever leave her barren.

The trauma and loss rendered the thought of another man ever touching her out of the question. Despite what her eyes had seen and her body endured during her captivity, her giving ways and bright eyes continued to tell of her former self. So it came to pass that she would give what was left of herself to helping kids who, like her, for no reason but race were not given a chance.

During the years of their relationship, there was always enough to do around Greta's house to keep Al in pocket money. As he became older, Al's labors at the house stopped being for money and became labors of love. Love for a house, love for the product of his labor, and most of all love for an aging woman who had become his confidant and friend.

Anthony D. Carr

When Greta died, no one was more surprised than Al that he was invited to the reading of his friend's will. Attending were two ancient Jewish attorneys and Al.

His friend had left everything that she had, except her house, to his future children. Who would have ever guessed that she was worth well over seven million dollars? Arrangements were set up to care and educate his children and see to all of their needs.

Never one to give someone something for nothing — "They just don't appreciate it," she would say — her will gave Al the opportunity to buy her house and everything in it for one $150,000. The house was a bargain at that price since it was worth about four times that amount.

After pulling his resources together, which included his UPS stock that had recently made many employees able to live comfortably, he could just make it. He came up with the money, and the house was his. If only he had known what would happen to his baby's mama. If only Terow had known that O'ne would be taken care of.

♩ ♩ ♩

Safely inside of the house, Al cued up Miles Davis' "So What." The song embodied how he had been feeling over the past few months. During that time, he had come to rely on the song's lyrics more and more each day. It was becoming easy to set his day's events to the song's beat.

Al didn't go to work today — So what!

Dead Roots Wilting Flower

Listened to music all day — So what!
Got this big old house — So what!
No one to love it but me — So what!
Now they want to take my O'ne ...

 The next "So what" would never come out of him. He knew that he had to fight those who wanted to control O'ne's trust and those who wanted to take his place and raise his daughter. Her mother had already paid the ultimate sacrifice. He had to do what was in his heart. He had to do what was right.

Chapter 8

Al rang the doorbell for the third time and was getting upset. Just after his first ring, he saw someone come to the broken front window of the brown-brick bungalow and try to sneak a look to see who was ringing the bell.

"If they think they are going to avoid me and keep me from O'ne they are mistaken," Al thought to himself as he depressed the doorbell button and leaned on it for an extended ring.

Seconds later, the door swung open and Terow's father, Mr. Clark, and his grown son Freddie appeared in the doorway.

Dead Roots Wilting Flower

"Hello Mr. Clark. How are you? Do you have a few minutes to talk?" Al heaved it all out of his mouth in one breath.

"I don't see that we have anything else to talk about. Like I told you before, you weren't around before she died so there's no reason for you to come around now."

Mr. Clark's voice was stern and possessed an unyielding quality.

"Yeah! What the hell do you want now? You want to be daddy," Freddie mocked, poking his chest out of the doorway then walking out past Al and behind him.

Al found himself with one man in front of him and one man behind him. With the way they were positioned, he couldn't keep his eyes on both of them. Al turned to the side and did the best he could to stay out of harm's way.

"Is it possible that I can at least see O'ne?" Al insisted.

"No, it's best that you don't. We can talk right here," Mr. Clark asserted strongly.

As Mr. Clark spoke, he gave Al a look that implied he was lower then trash. They blamed him for a death that he would have given his own life to have avoided.

"It's getting dark out here and this isn't the safest of neighborhoods," Al offered, in hopes of getting into the house to see his child.

"Don't worry, I run this here," Freddie said walking a little closer into Al's personal space. "You're OK for right now."

Instinctively, Al put his hand on his waist, feeling a false sense of comfort knowing that his five-shot derringer was just inches away from his fingertips. Al knew better than to come into Chicago's Gresham neighborhood looking for a fight. The pistol that he carried was a just-in-case measure.

"Mr. Clark, all I am asking is that I be allowed to raise my child," Al calmly said.

"You can raise all of your children. This one here, you don't have any right to. Anything that she needs, I'll see to. It's too late for you."

Raising his voice, Al responded to Mr. Clark. "You raised your children. Would you have allowed someone else to raise a child of yours?"

"That's different. Like I said, this one here is not yours," Mr. Clark retorted.

"It seems like you don't have any more business here," Freddie said to Al with a slight threat in his voice.

"What?" Al exclaimed without thinking.

Freddie, feeling that it was time for him to take charge, moved in.

"Look man, I don't think that it's safe for you over here any more. It's time for you to leave."

Al knew that it was best for him to heed this young man's warning. Al also knew that his resolve was being tested by these two men, and to back away completely now would mean that next time they would come down even harder on him.

His manhood at issue, Al responded, "All right I'll leave, but this is far from over."

"Hey, whatever you want I can oblige," Freddie said, hitting his chest with his fist in a show of masculinity.

Al moved quickly to his car without saying another word. Once inside his car, the gravity of the situation hit him. These guys were willing to hurt him. He was going to have to fight on two fronts if he was going to get his little girl. He had to stand tall for what was right. What kind of father would allow someone else to raise his child?

Al drove down Ashland Avenue thinking about what his next move should be. He had to find out what he was up against with Freddie Clark. Reluctantly, Al decided to seek out an element that he never thought he would need again. In his youth, Al ran with a few of the Gresham neighborhood movers and shakers. However, after being away from the hood for so long he didn't know who to trust. Al decided to ask a source with whom he had an extended history.

Al walked into "The Room." The Room was a barber shop where you could get one of the best haircuts and shaves in the city of Chicago — as well as anything else you were looking for. For the right price anything was available, including the best drugs, information, and street influence.

Glancing around the shop, Al noticed that most of the faces of the men cutting hair in the shop's ten barber stations had changed. The one face that hadn't changed was that of the man talking the loudest in the shop's first chair by the window.

"The Bulls ain't going to be shit again this year," the loud man boasted in a voice that fit his over-four-hundred-pound frame.

"Yeah, but I bet you that Jordan has those Wizards ready," someone in the room replied.

"Big Dave," Al called to the large man.

"Yeah, that's me. Who that?" the big man asked, straining to bring Al into focus.

"D, it's me, Al. Al from back in the day."

The blood drained from the heavyset man's face and it looked like he just saw a ghost.

"Take your ass in the back, boy."

Excusing himself from his client, the heavy man wasted no time ushering Al into the invitation only back room.

"What in the hell are you doing here?" The big man asked in a surprisingly soft and quiet voice for a man so big.

"What do you mean?"

"Man, there's ten large on your head."

"What?"

"Yeah, man. You need to stay out of the hood for a while. You know things aren't organized like they used to be. Bunch of cowboys out here now."

"Who put the money up?"

"It's Freddie's pops, man. The crew they got is only good here in the hood. You should be OK if you don't fuck around over here."

"Thanks, man. I owe you one," Al gratefully replied and slapped Dave's hand.

Al was on his way out the door when Dave called after him.

"Al, use the back way. I can't take the heat. I ain't as young as I used to be so, it's best that you don't come back here anymore. Sorry man."

"Naw Big D. I understand."

With that, Al carefully made his exit.

Chapter 9

After four weeks on the job, Kayla was mentally exhausted, sitting in her bedroom after a long day. The honeymoon at the job was over. She was now being given projects to oversee and timely status reports to the Mayor and City Council members were expected.

Outside of the demands of the job, having more of an effect were the little changes that were starting to occur. There was nothing that she was able to do about them, so she resolved to just deal with them. Thinking about the changes, she started talking to her joy and rubbing her mid-section.

Just as she lay her head on her down-filled pillow, the phone rang.

"Hello ... Hi, mama how are you? ... I feel fine but the visions have started again ... No! mama, I can't just run home to you whenever I see something ... Yes, ma, I know that you are there for me. Don't worry, mama, I found a good doctor that I'm comfortable with and I'm trying to control it ... No ma, it's a little different this time. The visions seem so real. It's kind of scary ... No, I've already made up my mind ... I'm not coming back to Alabama ... No, I'm not stressed out over James ... Look, James had his chance. He made his choice, and now we're going to live with it ... Mama this is two thousand and three. Women do things differently now ... Can we stop this conversation? I'm not going to change my mind. James is history and he does not deserve any information about us ... I know what's best for us, mama ..."

༄ ༄ ༄

Esteen Wright is not the kind of woman that takes a "no" sitting down. Over the years, as a single mother, to nurture her family she had to be a "take charge" type of woman. She was especially that way when it came to her daughter Kayla. Even being so far away, she still felt like she had to do something. Something to help. Something to make sure that her child didn't do anything that she would be sorry for the rest of her life.

It didn't go unnoticed by Esteen that her daughter's health was at its best when she was with James. James was the one for her daughter. She just knew it.

Before the imprint of the telephone receiver could disappear from her ear, Esteen's mind was made up as to what she was going to do. The only question was how to do it. Finding James would not be too much of a problem. However, what she was going to say to him once she called him was a different matter. How much of her daughter's business could she reveal without crossing the line? The line that when crossed by a family member risks the relationship with the very person they are trying to help.

ʒ ʒ ʒ

"Hello, information .... New York, New York please ... James Anderson ... No, I don't know the address but I do know his middle initial ... It's "Z" as in zebra ... Can you repeat that? ... No! I mean that's OK, I will to call later. Thank you ... Goodbye."

The nervousness that Esteen felt was a surprise to her. She had felt compelled to intervene in her daughter's life before and for the most part she had gained pretty good results. But she had never done anything that was this important before, mind you. What else could she do? She couldn't let her daughter walk out on a future, could she?

Esteen wished that her daughter had a little more of her fight in her. "Maybe things come too easy for her?" Esteen's mind drifted further into what her daughter was doing with her life. It's not often that you find a good man willing to accept a woman with an illness. Especially an illness like hers. "Fight for that man," she wanted to scream at her daughter.

Her resolve strengthened. She thought, "All she needs is someone to light a match under her butt, that's all."

She could not believe that her hands were shaking as she stood there with the phone in them.

"Too late to turn back," she said to herself as she pushed the buttons of the Touch Tone phone.

A heavy voice answered on the third ring. "Hello."

Phone in her hand, ready to do what had to be done, hands shaking, words, the right words that were in her head, would not come into her mouth. Mrs. Wright had no choice but to hang up the phone without saying a word.

"What's wrong with me? Why couldn't I speak to that boy?"

After a little thought, she decided to call a little later after she had a couple of Miller Lites to calm her nerves.

ʒ ʒ ʒ

James was wide awake, wishing that he could turn back the hands of time. He was living the old saying, "You don't miss your water until your well runs dry." Kayla was the water that he didn't even know he needed until it was too late.

"Damn, damn, damn, how in the hell did I get myself into this mess?" James thought, continuing to quietly beat himself up for his past mistake.

"How did I not know better? I didn't know that I loved Kayla this way," he thought to himself.

"I let her go for this?" James asked himself as he lay next to the one he had left Kayla for. It was true that

Dead Roots Wilting Flower

Kayla did not boast the social pedigree that he wanted. James was guilty of thinking too much of what he had to have if he was going to marry a woman. He had been thinking with his second head, his wallet and potential social standing instead, of with his heart.

Gone were the nights of being awakened by a gentle tug that silently said, "I want you now." Those nights were now replaced with a restlessness that stemmed from being unfulfilled both physically and mentally.

James looked over at his partner in peaceful sleep and knew that the person sleeping there was not feeling what he was feeling. That same glance made clear in his mind that he could not go on like this. James was unhappy and needed his girl back.

James eased out of the bed and went into his study. There he found a piece of paper and started writing.

I'm sorry for what I've done. I don't want to lose that special someone. I miss you...

In seconds, the paper was flooded with tears. James was paying a heavy price for pushing love aside.

Chapter 10

"Hey, Kayla," Al called after her.

Al was surprised to see Kayla in the Freeman building.

"Al," Kayla replied after turning around. Her voice filled with surprise and just a hint of discomfort.

"It's good to see you. What are you doing down here?"

"I have a five o'clock appointment."

"Girl, you're way too early. It's not even three thirty."

"Yeah, I know, but it's such a beautiful day that I just wanted to get out into it," she replied, still visibly uncomfortable.

"Well, I just finished up my appointment. Doctors! They know how to bring you down. Do you want to kill some time before your five o'clock?"

"I don't care, Al," Kayla dryly replied.

"Man, you sure know how to make a guy feel wanted. I don't want to intrude."

"No, Al, I didn't mean it like that. It's just that, just that there are a few things on my mind," Kayla said choosing her words carefully. "Yeah, why not. Come on, let's hang if you think you can keep up with me."

Kayla lightened up after she accepted Al's offer. They went for ice cream and then on, Al's suggestion, they walked over to the Reading Room, an Afrocentric bookstore on State Street. While there, Al enjoyed watching the selection of books that caught Kayla's attention. Al observed that she picked up a lot of self-help books.

Over the ensuing ninety minutes, they enjoyed some good clean fun as they talked about little things and became closer friends. As their time together was winding down and the time for Kayla to see Dr. King started to draw near, she decided to take a leap of faith and ask Al to do her a big favor.

"Al, can you do me a favor if you have the time?" Kayla asked abruptly, ending a very comfortable silence between them as they walked down Madison Avenue.

"OK. No problem. What is it?"

"Before you say OK, you'd better hear what it is," she warned.

"Woman, I'm not worried. Lay it on me." "Woman" is what Al had been calling Kayla all afternoon. By this time, although she didn't know it, Al would have walked a country mile just to spend more time with her.

Without hesitation, Kayla jumped in with both feet and began, "Al, I've been seeing a therapist about a problem I have been unable to shake for most of my life."

After her revelation, she became hesitant and waited for a response from Al.

"Just like a man," she thought to herself, "loud when he shouldn't be and quiet when you need him to say something."

When Al didn't respond, Kayla continued. "I'm on my way to see him now and it always wears me out. I was wondering if you could go with me? I mean if you're not too busy or anything."

"What's the doctor's name that you're seeing?"

"King, Dr. King," she revealed.

"Woman, you're not going to believe this. I've been seeing him too. I haven't been able to get over the death of my baby's mama," Al told Kayla in a no-big-deal tone.

"Small world, huh," Kayla said in a small voice.

"Yeah. A small world and a funny world isn't it? Who would have thought that we would be here in the middle of downtown bonding?"

"Come on boy, I have to go. I assume that since you have a relationship with the good doctor, you will be coming with me?" she lightheartedly inquired.

"Bet," Al said with no hesitation.

Al was ecstatic at how Kayla and he were vibing. He glanced over at her from the corner of his eyes and saw the same woman that he had viewed over a month ago from the window. He knew that he could never tell her that he had seen into her world. No way. He had to play it cool and keep his personal wants and desires to himself.

Walking toward Dr. King's office, Kayla felt remarkably close to Al. It was as if he knew her inner self. Once inside the Freeman Building, the tightness in the pit of her stomach reminded her that now was not the time to be having thoughts about some man. Besides, Len and Al were friends, and Len was still trying.

"I wonder what their attitudes would be if they knew," Kayla allowed herself to imagine as they left the elevator and approached the office door.

"No, I'm not going there. It would be new city — same old bull. By myself is best. By myself is what it is. We don't need anybody," Kayla continued to think silently even while signing in at the reception desk.

In a few minutes she knew that her world would be somewhere back in time and she would have no earthly idea how she mentally got there.

Her recent sessions with Dr. King were troubling. She at least expected to feel good after paying good money to see a therapist who was there to help her. However, she had been leaving her appointments with Dr. King mentally and physically drained, encumbered with thoughts that she was unable to explain.

Dead Roots Wilting Flower

"At least this time I won't be alone after the session," Kayla happily thought. "I hope Al can take away any lingering thoughts of the past that stay with me."

The session lasted exactly one hour, as prescribed. When Kayla opened her eyes, she was surprised to see fresh stains of perspiration in the armpits of Dr. King. She was used to her own clamminess after a session with this doctor, but this was the first time that Dr. King had looked spent afterward.

"Ms. Wright, that was intense. How do you know these things? Did someone tell them to you?"

"No, Dr. King, they just come to me like the clearest TV program you ever saw. You know, the funny part is that while it's happening, I feel like I'm really there."

"What about the young lady. Do you know her?"

"I don't know, Dr. King."

"You know that you can tell me anything, and if we need to we can call the police. I'll be right here with you."

"I don't know her. All I know is that I did my best to help her and not let it happen. There were just too many of them. They knocked me down, I hit my head, and then I couldn't get back up," Kayla remembered out loud.

As she spoke, Kayla reached back behind her head to the area that hit the ground in her vision and was not surprised to find that her head was tender in the spot where she fell in her memory. Many times after she recalled something in the distant past, she would find physical signs of her mental adventure.

"They hurt her. It was one man after another. I couldn't do anything. I'm just one man."

The word "man" came out of Kayla's mouth without her awareness. The fact that she continued to use the word meant that Kayla was still in her thoughts.

"You mean just one woman, don't you, Kayla?"

Kayla didn't answer. She was a bit confused. As usual, Dr. King had no answers and provided her with little comfort. She stayed with him because, unlike the others, he was able at least to get into her thoughts. The others felt that medication was the only answer. Right now, taking medication for her condition was not an option; the thoughts in her head had to be faced head-on.

Dr. King was beginning to teach her how to stop fighting the memories and just let them flow through her. Unfortunately, an unwanted byproduct of this approach of letting her thoughts run free was that thoughts of James were also coming into her mind more and more.

With medication ruled out, Kayla routinely turned to talking to someone deeply or seeing a good movie where she could lose herself in the plot and stem the flow of memories of things that she had not actually experienced. She still had to be careful; the wrong movie or conversation could all by itself start her memories back into motion.

Today, she had Al to lean on. She knew it was wrong not to tell him what was going on, but she really needed him and didn't want to scare him off with something that would surely seem crazy to him.

Al was waiting for Kayla after the appointment, as promised. For some reason she didn't expect him to be. Maybe that would explain the wide smile and enthusiasm with which she met him. Al was just happy to be in her company. With their smiles brightly shining, the two of them looked like they were in need of mental help as they left Dr. King's office.

The conversation in the car during the short ride to Kayla's Dearborn Park townhouse revolved around why Al was seeing Dr. King. Al's issues of guilt were intense, and Kayla's heart rapidly went out to his motherless little girl, O'ne.

"Your daughter has already lost her mother and now it's a fight between the people that should only be loving her," Kayla said sadly to Al.

"Yeah, I know, but what can I do? Give up? I've already bent over backward for them. I've given them every assurance that I will never take their grandchild out of their lives. It just seems that they want to break me."

"Al, she's your child and no matter what happens nothing can change that."

"I know but this fight is taking everything that I mentally have."

"Just hang in there, OK?" Kayla offered as words of support.

"You have no idea how much my life has changed since the accident three months ago. Hell, this is the first time in my adult life that I don't have a love interest. It's all too strange."

"Yes you do, Al," Kayla replied.

"Do what?"

"Have a love interest."

Al looked at her questioningly, wondering if she already knew about his feelings for her or his interloping into her life. His puzzled look caused her to speak again.

"You do have a love interest. I can see it when you talk to me. You love that little girl more than you love yourself. It would be easy to just walk away, but you are still fighting."

"You're right. There's more love in my heart than there ever has been."

Al hoped that his statement about not having a love interest would open a door to their getting together but in the seconds that followed he saw that he had gotten much more than he expected. He knew that it was best that the door to Kayla's heart did not open. Inside himself he knew that with his current problems he wasn't any good for any woman.

Kayla, after hearing Al talk, realized that everyone had issues. The realization was comforting to her; she knew that she wasn't alone in her agony and that if others could bear it, then she could too.

Before either one of them was ready, Al was parked in front of her carless garage saying an awkward goodbye.

"Al, why don't you come in and see my new place?" Kayla offered, more for herself than for Al.

"OK. I have a minute or two."

Once inside of Kayla's townhouse, the first thing that hit Al was how finished and home-like the townhouse was even though she had only being there a few months.

"You've only been in Chicago three months?" Al inquired. "It looks like you've been here for years. I just moved four months ago and my house is a wreck."

"Well, I just wanted to be comfortable as quickly as possible. You know how easy it is to get homesick. It was hard enough leaving New York. Putting this place together kept my mind off the Big Apple."

Al, knowing things that he should not, couldn't help himself when he inquired, "What in the Big Apple did you need your mind taken off of?"

Kayla reflected for a moment and then went blank. Just like that, she was back in time.

ა ა ა

James and Kayla had just enough time to make it to the New Year's Eve party before it turned into a New Year's Day party. They pulled up to the valet at the Double Tree Inn when the dash board clock read eleven thirty-six. For the price of a five-dollar tip, the valet attendant instructed them on the quickest way up to the two-bedroom presidential suite that James' brother had reserved for the evening's festivities.

The party was a gathering of select friends that knew how to move and shake things up in and around the city.

Entering the room, it didn't take Kayla long to realize that she didn't know anyone other than James and his brother, Philip. It was also odd to her that, on a night when most people are coupled up, of the thirty or so people that were there, more than twenty were men.

Philip took the time, as the clock ticked down the old year, to introduce James and Kayla around the room full of notables. The room was filled with many of the city's up and coming movers and shakers. The introductions included "aid to this so-and-so", "vice president of this", "head of that." Every now and again they would be introduced to a trophy wife or girlfriend that had accompanied one of the big headed men to the party. During the introductions, it also became clear that there were only couples in the room.

At about five to the hour, Kayla thought it best to go to the bathroom before everyone else wanted to go there after the new year came in. She leaned over and told James her intentions, and she didn't think twice about his offer to accompany her.

They both entered the bathroom. The door was closed and its lock was turned. Kayla leaned over the vanity to check her face.

James, turning from the door, was treated to a striking view of ass and legs. From where he stood, due to the way she was bending over the sink to apply her makeup, he could see the top of Kayla's stockings and the clips on the bottom of her garters. With that backdrop, there was no warning giving. There was just an animalistic attack.

In an instant he was pressed against her backside. It only took one motion for him to rip her lacy, little more than a thong, panties from their job of covering what was hers to give and his for the taking.

Kayla stood fast with physical and mental anticipation. It's always better when two people want the same thing, and when it came to sex, Kayla always wanted James. The very next instant filled and fulfilled her physical anticipation. James was surprised at just how ready she was. She was wet, hot, and ready.

In this exchange there were no words, just action. Hard action so unrefined, that had anyone been looking on, they would question if this act were consensual.

Kayla stood fast and moaned softly within. She held all audible sound inside of her until she heard the people outside the door counting down the seconds of the old year.

"Ten, nine, eight . . ."

She knew that James thought that he was getting the best of her.

"Five, four, three," the countdown continued.

At the count of three, she clenched tight everything that she had. Between three and two it was clear that James could not hold himself much longer. At two she was in control for the first time. While still clenched tight, she forced her weight onto her heels and drove her hips back onto him. Three quick instantaneous hip movements followed.

"Happy New Year, happy . . ."

By the third happy New Year, James exploded. The throbbing nature of the explosion coupled with the heat of the released fluid was the catalyst for her release. It was done. Sex without an expression of love was taxing, but the relief was worth the effort.

Washcloth in hand, Kayla tried to wash away the noticeable aura of sex that abounded in the hopes of returning to the party and acting as if nothing had happened. It wasn't any time to really cleanse herself to her satisfaction — some things require you to put that thing in some water. The most that she could do with the washcloth was to wipe the beads of sweat from her forehead.

The night was over, at least here at the party. Who knows once they arrived home.

༄ ༄ ༄

"Kayla, wake up! Are you OK?" Al asked, happy to see her eyes opening.

Al was close to calling 911 when Kayla's eyes began to respond to his urging. Kayla's eyes, slowly opening, found Al standing over her dabbing her forehead with a cool, wet, towel picking up tiny beads of sweat. The wet towel on her forehead was too much like the past. She had to gather all of her inner strength not to go back to where she had just been.

After a few moments, when she was close to getting it together, she became aware that she had lost her shower. This was the second time in a few hours that she had intensely sweated. Once in Dr. King's office and now.

Dead Roots Wilting Flower

Sweat on a clean body is OK. Sweat on a body that has already sweated, no way. Getting up from the floor, she noticed that she was extremely wet between her legs.

"How long was I out, Al?" She questioned.

"Less then a minute, but you scared the mess out of me."

"Sorry. That's what I was trying to tell you — I have issues," Kayla said in an apologetic voice.

"Hey, woman, we all have them, but even with them, your friends stick around. I'll be around," Al assured.

They sat on the couch for a few minutes until Al sensed that it was time to exit. Kayla was uncomfortable about the loss of her shower and was ready for Al to leave so that she could do something about it.

Before he rose from the couch, Al wrote his home phone number on the back of someone else's business card that he found in the recesses of his wallet.

Al passed Kayla the card, allowing his hand to touch hers and linger to get his point across.

The moment was tenured when he said, "If you need me, call me. All right?"

"OK, but you don't have to worry about me."

"Whatever," Al said with a sigh. "You mean that after what I just saw you can sit there and tell me not to worry? Right! Bye woman, and you keep my number close," Al commanded and hoped at the same time.

Chapter 11

"Hello? ... This is James Anderson ... How are you, Ms. Wright? I'm glad you called. I've wanted to get in touch with Kayla since she left town ... No, I don't have an address or phone number for her ... Of course I care about her. I just, I mean, I made a big mistake ... Chicago? You mean she moved all the way to Chicago? ... No, Ms. Wright, I'm not asking you to get in the middle of this. I just want to be able to talk to her and tell her how I really feel about her ... Ms. Wright this is all my fault; not hers at all ... I would like to tell her; I mean she doesn't know that I just recently realized how much I care about your daughter ... I won't cause any trouble ... Hold on a second and let me get a pen. OK, I'm ready ... I got it. That's

312.555.5789. Thank you, Ms. Wright, I won't let you down ... I understand and thanks again ... Bye."

James sat with the phone and Kayla's phone number in his lap debating what he should do next. He was searching his mind, trying to find a way to explain his past actions to her and not lose her for good. Forty-five minutes later, still siting in the same position, it came to him that this was not something he could do over the phone; he needed to be in Chicago.

James picked up the phone and quickly dialed American Airlines reservations. After being on hold for more than five minutes, someone came on the line.

"... Hello Jennifer operator eight, OK ... I need to know the availability of flights from New York to Chicago ... Today, right now if possible, and I need the return to be open ... Six hundred seventy-five! OK, that will be fine. Can I pick that ticket up at the airport along with a one way ticket from Chicago to New York? ... The round trip passenger's name is Anderson, James Anderson ... Yes, I am an Advantage member. Can you look up my number? ... The one-way passenger will be Kayla Wright ... That's flight 1819, leaving Kennedy today at 6:45 and arriving in Chicago at 8:17 ... Yes, I do need a car at the airport ... full-size is fine ... Thank you for everything Jennifer, operator eight. Bye."

James clicked the button on the cordless phone and gazed into open space. More than four months had passed since things exploded between them. Sitting here now, he hoped that once he saw her and got her back in his arms everything would be OK.

ℑ ℑ ℑ

Al sat outside courtroom 1603 in Chicago's Daley Center in the heart of downtown frantically trying to reach his attorney on his cell phone. His case had been passed over three times in the last two hours while they waited for Attorney Goodman to arrive. Not only was his case being jeopardized, but he was expected to arrive to work at 3:30 and it was already 3:00.

"These damn attorneys. Their time is so precious that they can charge two hundred fifty dollars an hour, but when it comes to jacking off a few hours of *your* time, they act like it's no big deal," Al mumbled under his breath.

"Eight court appearances, seventeen thousand dollars in attorneys' fees and we are still on square one," he continued to think.

It wouldn't be so bad except that each time he came to this courtroom his expectations were so high. Each time, after leaving the courtroom, his emotions were so low that they needed to be scraped off of the floor.

Attorney Goodman finally brushed into the courtroom and made a beeline to the Judge's clerk. A few sentences were mouthed between them before he walked back to Al and motioned for him to follow him into a conference room off to the side of the courtroom.

"I'm sorry, Al, but I was held over in federal court on another matter," Goodman explained, with a very concerned look on his face. "Your case has been continued for thirty days."

"They must make attorneys practice these sorry-assed speeches and looks in law school," Al began. "You don't what it does to me you understand every time something like this happens? No! You and your kind have no idea what it's like to be on the other side, do you?"

Al was letting Goodman know exactly what was on his mind.

"You have to understand that I have other clients too," Goodman replied.

"You need to understand! Understand what it's like to think that today might be the day your daughter will be withheld from you, and not knowing if you will ever get to be in her life. No Attorney Goodman, I don't think *you* understand!"

All the strain of the last four months was in Al's words.

Goodman approached Al to put his hand on his shoulder. Al put his hand up, stopping Goodman in his tracks.

"I want you to imagine how you would feel if someone took your child away from you for no good reason. How hard would you work then? Would you have been two hours late to court. Could you reconcile yourself another month without your child?"

"Al, you have to understand that these things hap . . ."

Al cut him off in mid-sentence. "Don't worry about it Attorney Goodman. Clearly, you have too many other cases on your plate. From this point on you can take this one off of it."

"Don't be so hasty, Al. I know that you're upset. I'll motion the case up next week and we'll get some movement then."

If things could get any worse, they did. O'ne's grandfather, Mr. Clark, stomped up to where the two men were standing. The ease to his step was such that he didn't require the cane that he held in his right hand.

"Do you give up yet?" the older man asked with a smug smile peaking through the hard look on his face.

Al did his best to respect the older man by ignoring him so that nothing out of the way came out of his mouth. With the way he was feeling, it was possible that he might hit Mr. Clark in his smug face.

"You know we don't have to go through any of this. We can take it to the streets and settle this right now. Last man standing." Mr. Clark dug deeper into Al.

"Whatever you want old man. Whatever you want," Al growled into his enemy's face.

"I think that it's best that you leave, Mr. Clark," Attorney Goodman calmly requested.

After Mr. Clark walked away, Al turned his attention back to Goodman.

"You still don't understand, do you?" Al asked in a sarcastic tone. "You've had four months to pimp me. That's four months to charge for your time, phone calls, and letters that have gotten us nowhere. I'm well done and you're fired."

"What?" The look on Goodman's face was one of shear surprise.

"Goodbye, Mr. Goodman. By the way, I don't expect to be billed for today." Al walked away with more uncertainty ahead.

ʒ ʒ ʒ

The light music was not too loud in the background. It was not enough of a distraction to take his mind away from the task at hand. Now, at five in the morning, Al had spent the last seven hours surfing the net and reading everything he could find about fathers' rights.

Knowledge is a powerful thing. The articles that he read were enlightening and calming at the same time. It became clear to him that his right to raise O'ne was well-grounded in law and the moral fabric of this country.

The more he read, the more he regretted his choice of Attorney Goodman. What Al needed was somebody who specialized in this type of case. It was also clear to him that Goodman, a white man, had no connection to the unique issues facing a black father or to what O'ne's grandparents might be feeling after the loss of a daughter. For that matter, Goodman had not a clue as to how an extended family functions in a minority community.

No, Goodman was not the right man for the job and finding a replacement was going to take some investigation and thought. Al planned on beginning that search with the Cook County Bar Association, which is the Chicagoland association for black lawyers. He hoped that his next attorney would be a competent, strong black person who had the compassion to understand the importance of the task at hand.

When this thing first started, Al was referred to mostly white Jewish attorneys. People recommended them highly because it was thought that they had the extra pull that a minority attorney could not provide. However, in today's times, trading on influence is less effective than knowing what you are doing.

"I won't make the same mistake twice," Al assured himself.

Al was just finishing reading "In Re the Matter of Harris", the latest United States Supreme Court case outlining that a parent's right to raise his child outweighs a grandparent's right to intervene. In Al's mind, the cases were clear. It was time for action. No more Mr. Nice Guy.

ʓ ʓ ʓ

"Why is this woman sleeping next to me?" Len silently thought to himself. His eyes were wide shut as he did his best to remain motionless in his waterbed. He hadn't planned this. He had such high expectations for this evening before it started.

He set up his date with Kayla over a week ago. All that was left for her to do was to confirm what time he was to pick her up. He had it all planned. Pick her up and enjoy a cozy dinner at Shaws Crab House. After dinner he was going to take her out for a night of dancing at Chicago's Original First Fridays.

Len knew that at this monthly party his crew would be there giving him support to ensure that Kayla knew he was The Man. Additionally, introducing her to his friends as his girlfriend would be a good way to start shedding his current lifestyle of juggling two, sometimes three women at the same time.

In anticipation of the date, Len purchased an arrangement of tropical flowers from Blossoms of Hawaii, a surprisingly affordable Michigan Avenue florist that he had used for many years. The vividly colored arrangement of flowers was very different from the under-appreciated, overused roses that many men, without much thought, give to women every day.

The richly colored flowers made a statement that set Len apart from the rank and file. Len added his personal touch by requesting two bird of paradise flowers in the array. He wanted the two flowers to symbolize the paradise he knew that he and Kayla could experience if only she would relax and let things flow between the two of them.

By nine, it was clear that Kayla was not going to call. Len, true to form, picked up the phone and arranged for a companion for the evening. It was not going to be the night he expected, but he needed to take the edge off of being snubbed.

Gloria asked the doorman to ring Len's phone from the lobby of the Presidential Towers apartment building.

"... Send her up please ... Thank you."

Dead Roots Wilting Flower

Len waited the two minutes that it took Gloria to ascend thirty-two floors by elevator and find his apartment with a numbness about him. He knew that he would only be going through the motions since, in his mind, Gloria could never be the one.

Throughout his dating history, Len always set boundaries with the women he dated. Usually, in just a few minutes, and most assuredly after the first date was over, Len would know in his heart how far he wanted the relationship to go. In most cases, he limited his expectations of a woman to nothing more than friend or sexual partner.

From the beginning it was different with Kayla. When he met her, he didn't feel the need to place her in some category. The relationship just grew and, without his knowledge or consent, engulfed him. During the first few months, everything between Kayla and him was great, and she emotionally moved deeper and deeper into his mind with a speed heretofore unknown to him.

Like a balloon filled with hydrogen reacting to a lighted match, the relationship exploded. In the end, for the first time in his life, Len was left broken. The pain of being rejected and broken was just too much for him. He had to do something about it. It didn't take long for him to start mending himself with the opposite sex.

Gloria knocked on the door and Len opened it.
"Hey, Gloria, how are you?"

"Good," she replied as she moved closer to Len forcing him into a hello kiss.

Gloria kissed him deeply and passionately while Len only allowed himself to be kissed. He wanted to be kissed. Kissed with enough allure to erase the thoughts of what he could not have.

"Sit down and make yourself comfortable. I have a surprise for you," Len apprised her.

Knowing what he needed and the effect that flowers can have on a woman, Len decided without hesitation to give her the arrangement of flowers that he had purchased for someone else.

In the kitchen, Len retrieved the paper-wrapped flowers from the bottom of the refrigerator. Using the small amount of conscience that he had left, he removed one of the bird of paradise stems from the arrangement and calmly placed it in the trash disposal. He showed no emotion as he flipped the switch and eradicated the once beautiful cutting.

Back in the living room, flowers in hand, Len continued his mission to find relief from his mental pain. He was all smiles when he handed the flowers to Gloria.

"Oh, Len, these are gorgeous."

"I'm glad you like them," Len said with a put-on smile.

"Like them? I love them," she said, with a smile as big as Texas on her face. "Come here and let me show you how much I like them."

If physical pleasure were all that Len required to heal what ailed him, tonight he would be given a clean bill of health. Be that as it may, like a baby that only can be pacified with his favorite toy — any toy just would not do — Gloria was not Kayla and Len would not be cured this night.

Lying still in bed, Len opened his eyes and looked at the clock. "Five past five," he made a mental note. With no emotional desire to perform for Gloria again, he remained as still as possible so as not to arouse her.

Listening to her breathing patterns for a few minutes, Len ascertained that she was fast asleep. With that, he ventured to ease out of bed. His movements resulted in a slight ripple within the almost waveless waterbed mattress they were lying on. He was in luck. The motion was not enough to wake her.

Successfully removing himself from bed, Len went into the living room and settled onto the couch. The couch's oversized pillows were enough for him to close his eyes and imagine that it was Kayla and not a pillow beside him. With his mind where he wanted it to be, Len drifted into a restful sleep and an intimate dream.

Len heard the familiar music of Sports Center coming from the living room's TV as he fell out of sleep, all the while struggling to keep his eyes closed. If he had his faculties about him, he would have remembered that Gloria was a sports fanatic. That fact continued to escape him as he began to unwillingly react to the smooth touch of expert fingers, soft lips, and a wet tongue.

His reaction to her was slow, and by the time his size was more than filling Gloria's mouth, he was already mumbling to himself. A few moments later, while still lodged between dream and reality, the word Kayla came out of his mouth.

"What did you call me?" Gloria questioned, dropping him from her mouth.

"Uh, What?"

"I said, what did you call me?"

Fully awake and exposed, Len struggled to find his Fruit of the Loom, out-of-fashion briefs to cover up his mis-spoken word. The undergarment nowhere to be found, he answered her with the naked truth.

"I don't know what I called you," Len replied.

"You called me Kayla! I heard you! Who in the hell is Kayla?"

Len thought about lying but decided against it since they were friends.

"She's someone I know. What difference does it make; we're only friends," Al offered in a calm voice.

"Oh, I get it. You give all your friends flowers and have sex with them. Of course! Then I must wake all of my friends up by sucking their dicks. Is that it?"

Gloria was being sarcastic and unpredictable.

"Look. I didn't ask you to do anything. It just happened. You're as much at fault as I am," Len stated defiantly.

Long moments of silence followed. It was all the time that Gloria needed to break two oversized vases and

Dead Roots Wilting Flower

shatter the glass panes in three framed prints. Before Len could fully comprehend what was happening, the door slammed to his bedroom. A few minutes later, she emerged fully dressed heading for the door.

Len didn't fully understand why she had the flowers he gave her snugged tightly under her arm. He resisted asking her why and also resisted trying to explain himself to her. He thought that it was best to let her leave before things became worse.

After she left, Len took a few moments to reflect on what had happened. He resolved that if he had just stayed the course and waited for Kayla to come to her senses none of this would have happened. As he laid his head back on the pillows of the couch, he wondered if it was too early to call Kayla.

Chapter 12

"Who is calling me this time of the morning?" Kayla asked herself while savoring the last sip of her morning coffee.

The coffee was strong, very strong, extra sweet, and don't forget the cream. Kayla liked her coffee just like she likes her men — strong, sweet, and light. She arrived to the phone's caller ID by the phone's third ring. By the fifth ring, Kayla had made up her mind that she was not going to answer. Two rings ago, Len's number had come up on the phone's caller ID.

"Lord, please not this morning," she spoke directly to the phone's caller ID box.

The phone continued to chime eight additional rings before it quit. A quiet "thank you" was softly spoken by her when the phone stopped in mid-ring. To her dismay Len called right back and let the phone ring ten additional times.

"I'm not trying to avoid Len," Kayla reassured herself mentally, "I'm just not in the mood to relive a past that is over; not this morning."

Kayla continued to try and sort through what she was feeling about Len. It came to her as she mixed sugar into her second cup of coffee. He was the right color and sweet as the day was long. Looking back over the course of their relationship, she decided that he just wasn't strong enough. She didn't think he was able to handle her issues. The second she began thinking that he could not cope, he became unacceptable to her. Now, facing even more problems, Kayla saw no logical reason to let him back into their life.

Notwithstanding how she felt about having a relationship with him, she did want Len to be her friend. She was sure that he could be a good one. However, whenever she opened the door to that friendship, Len pressed for more. Their prior history aside, Kayla knew that it was time for her to work on herself from within. She had to. When the time for family came, she would be ready.

Having thought through her Len issue to her satisfaction, she turned on the television. Flipping through the channels, she chose the Saturday Morning

Show. The show and its two woman anchors was a mix of breaking news and human interest stories.

Kayla quickly picked up on one of the stories and began talking back to the TV as was her normal way when she watched television or listened to talk radio. She was fully engulfed in the program when the Latino anchor woman announced the next story.

"Coming up next, right after the break, is our legal correspondent, noted Attorney William Johnson, who will be doing a segment on fathers' rights in the wake of the latest United States Supreme Court decision. Stay tuned."

Kayla moved quickly for the phone and dialed Al's number from memory. Over the last few weeks, she had used the number a lot, as she and Al were fast becoming good friends.

"... Al, this is Kayla. Sorry for calling so early but turn to Channel 16 ... No, they're about to have a segment on fathers' rights ... Good, and you're welcome ... OK, bye."

Al promised her that he would talk to her later that day. Placing the phone back into its cradle, Kayla thought to herself how good it felt talking to Al. With him there was never an ulterior purpose to their conversations. Their talks were always real and down to earth. Sitting back in front of the television, she thought about confiding in Al. Those thoughts slipped from her mind when the Saturday Morning Show resumed.

The ten-minute fathers' rights segment was filled with information on how courts have changed. No longer did fathers have to fight a presumption that they were not fit to have custody of their children.

During the program, a lot of attention was given to emphasizing that a natural parent's right to raise their child outweighed all third party rights unless he has done something outside of the child's best interests. At the end of the program, several hotline numbers were given along with the numbers of three national law firms that specialized in fathers' rights cases.

Throughout the show, Kayla took down notes on important points and wrote down the phone numbers at the end of the program just in case Al missed anything. When the segment was over, she thought about taping it.

"Why didn't I think of taping the show earlier?" she chastised herself.

She wasn't going to let anything bring her down. She felt good. The program didn't affect her life at all, just her friends, but she felt good all the same.

The rest of Kayla's morning, afternoon, and early evening were spent doing the rest and relaxation thing. Right now, in her condition, rest and relaxation was what the doctor ordered. During her long bath, she took care not to have her bath water boiling hot as she liked it. She also remembered to take her vitamins.

At 9:18 that night when the phone rang, Kayla felt like a new woman. A strong black woman who could face anything and anybody. She picked up the phone on its fourth ring, not bothering to check the caller ID.

Dead Roots Wilting Flower

"Hello ... James! how did you get this number?" With the question, her heart sank and the invincible feeling that she had moments ago was gone.

"... James, I can't do this right now! Can you call me back? ... In town! Chicago? ... No, I can't meet you for dinner. I just told you that now is not a good time ... You pop into town after dumping me and you expect me to drop everything? ... I can't promise you anything but I will try to call you. Is that OK? ... Well, it's the best I can do ... Goodbye, James."

Her strong forceful tone on the phone misrepresented her true state of mind. She was besides herself that James and her mother would conspire against her.

"James, well OK, I can see that; but mama; how could she?"

Kayla never put the phone down. There was a quick click, dial tone, and she was dialing Al's number.

"Al, this is Kayla. Can you call me back? It's important," she said into Al's answering machine.

Another click, dial tone, and speed dial.

"Mama, how could you; how could you?" She inquired on the verge of tears ... It's not your place to give out my number ... What all did you tell him? ... Look, you cannot run my life from a thousand miles away. In fact, you can't run my life at all."

Kayla slammed down the phone and curled herself into a ball on the couch and began to cry.

Al was on his was to pick-up a slab of ribs from Lims barbecue when his pager vibrated in the car's center console. The humming sound alerted him that he had a message waiting for him at home on his answering machine. His home phone was programmed to call his pager when a message was left. Al was in the habit of checking the messages as soon as they came in just in case the call had something to do with O'ne. It seemed like one of their mamas was always calling for one thing or another.

After picking up the message, he called Kayla.

"Hello, Kayla ... OK, I'll hold on ... Slow down, woman ... Take it easy, I'll be right there. I'm already in the car. Hold tight ... Ten minutes and I'm there; is that too soon? ... See you in a few."

Al heard in her voice that she needed somebody, and he wanted that somebody to be him. When he saw the flashing lights in his rear view mirror, he was more annoyed by the distraction from his current mission than worried at the possibility of getting a speeding ticket.

While pulling over, Al checked his memory and felt a sense of relief knowing that he had left his pistol at home and not clipped to his waist. When he bought the gun, he had vowed only to carry it when it was absolutely necessary. After he pulled over to the curb, the officer took her time approaching Al's car.

"I need to see your license and insurance, sir."

"I have them right here, officer."

Dead Roots Wilting Flower

It was a black policewoman in her late twenties. Through experience he knew that no amount of coyness or flirting was going to get him out of this jam. Al thought about telling her the truth and asking her for a break.

"Mr. Gold, you know that you were doing at least fifty-five in a forty-mile-per-hour zone, don't you," the officer inquired while reading the license and insurance card Al had given her.

To Al's trained ears, her words betrayed her. He knew that if she really knew how fast he was going she would have said so and not beat around the bush.

"She's looking for me to admit that I was speeding," Al thought to himself. Finally, he replied, "No officer, I couldn't have been going that fast."

"Mr. Gold, why don't you sit tight while I check things out?"

After about six minutes, Officer Williams — Al knew her name from the name plate pinned to her boyish looking chest — returned to his car.

Mr. Gold, I need you to slow down. It's Saturday night and we don't need any more statistics out here on the road.

"OK, Ms. Williams."

"That's Officer Williams, Mr. Gold," she corrected him, handing back his insurance card and license.

The officer walked back to her car and Al, knowing the drill, to avoid being pulled over a second time, reached over and grabbed the seat belt, in plain view of the

-121-

officer, and clicked the strap over his body. He then adjusted his rear view mirror, turned on his left turn signal, and slowly pulled away from the curb.

♋ ♋ ♋

"Come on in," Kayla dryly greeted Al at her townhouse door.

"Come on, woman, it can't be that bad. Can it?"

Not bothering to answer his question, she offered him a seat, not once looking directly at him. It didn't go unnoticed by Al that she was somewhere else. Another dead giveaway of her mental state was the deep blue, oversized man's shirt she had on. It was her only outer garment. The shirt fell to just below her mid-thigh while she was standing. Al had been to her house many times over the past month, and she was always dressed to the nines when he visited.

At ease as always with Kayla, Al comfortably sat back in a black velvet modern swivel rocking chair that gave him a view of the entire living room. Kayla uneasily sat Indian style on the couch across from him. The way that she was sitting, Al could not miss the vivid pink that revealed itself, from time to time, from beneath the hem of the blue shirt bottom.

To Al, between her legs was the most beautiful pink that he had ever seen. His imagination, coupled with the pink stimulation, caused him, in an instant, to be throbbing inside his black, loose-fitting cords. The situation made it clear to him that he was going to have to adjust himself or risk cutting off circulation to the family jewels. His physical state being urgent, he casually swiveled the chair, turning his body out of Kayla's view. Thinking that he was outside of her line of site — his reflection was clearly visible in the picture window that he sat in front of — he adjusted himself straight up inside of his Calvin Klein boxer briefs with a nonchalant movement of his hand.

Relief gained, Al turned the chair to face Kayla again. His lingering eyes betrayed him and made the situation clear to Kayla. The frown that had existed for the last two hours on her face was replaced with a smile. It was just what she needed. Knowing that the man she most wanted to want her could lust after her, even now in her physical and emotional condition, made her relax for the first time since she received James' call.

Kayla's grin was evident as she crossed her legs while pushing them to one side. She asked Al, "Why do men like my pink panties so?"

Al could feel his face turning red. "Look, woman, I'm only human."

"My fault; I'm sorry. I wasn't thinking about what I had on. Give me a second and I'll go change."

As she walked from the room, she couldn't help the continuing pleased feeling deep within herself of having had an effect on him. The slight dampness between her legs let her know that she had to be careful about what she allowed herself to think about.

In no time at all, she returned in a long, bright white terrycloth robe. The robe did its job of cooling off any lingering sexual reaction in both of them. The tone being set for conversation, Kayla began to tell Al about James. The comfort within her as she revealed her life to Al allowed her to talk freely to him.

"What is it with guys that one woman is not enough?" Kayla inquired, after telling Al how James had been seeing someone else while he was with her.

"I don't think all guys are like that. I really don't," Al offered.

"All I know is that I gave my all to him. What's so bad about it is that he told me every day that he loved me — and he still needed to be with someone else," Kayla said in a disgusted voice.

Al, remembering his friend Dee's words, offered, "A good friend of mine once said that he was taught that a man shouldn't try to settle down until there's nothing more important to him than his family. Maybe this James cat just hasn't gotten there yet."

"I don't know," she wearily replied.

"I know that it hurts, but I know for sure that all men don't stay like that. I mean, to be honest with you..." Al paused fearing that he was revealing too much of himself.

With caution thrown to the wind, he continued.

"For a long time I was like your ex. I regret it but I can't do anything about it now."

Kayla was surprised that a man, who seemed as caring as Al, was comparing himself to James, who had taken so much from her. Needing to know more, she sat and listened closely to him.

Dead Roots Wilting Flower

"Sometimes you love someone but don't know how to be a man about love. I remember when Dee changed his ways after he met Charity. We were at the club and Dee was uncharacteristically quiet and reserved. I asked him what was wrong. When he answered me, his eyes were aglow. He told me that there was nothing in the club that compared to what he already had. He told me that he didn't have to force himself to feel the way he did and be committed to her. He said it just happened; the commitment was just there."

Kayla, thinking about Al's words, felt her heart warm at the thought of being loved that hard.

"That's what I want. I want to feel safe giving my heart to someone. You know, I don't know if I can ever take a chance on giving my heart again," Kayla reflected.

"Do you know what I think?" Al asked, not expecting a reply.

"No what do you think, Al," Kayla sarcastically asked.

"OK, woman, watch yourself. You know I'm grown."

"Yeah, yeah, yeah; just tell me what you think, Al."

"Seriously! I think the pain that we go through is just getting us ready for the good part. Think about it. Don't bad relationships make us stronger and more ready to find that right relationship that will see us through? I'm sure of it. We're striving to get to the good part."

"No, that's not it for me. I'm just plain worn out. I can't see myself inviting pain into my life again. I'm just so finished."

With her response, Al felt a little bit of his hope for a relationship with Kayla slip from him.

Kayla's comfort level remained high and allowed her to tell Al about Len also.

"Why don't you tell both of them to get lost," Al inquired.

"James said that he's not going back to New York until I see him, and Len, you know how he is. Besides, I have some unfinished business with James."

"And that would be?" Al probed.

"Al, I've already told you enough for one day. Let's not get into that one, OK?"

"OK. We'll take this one step at a time. Let's get past tomorrow. One day at a time all right?"

"So, then, what do you suggest?"

"They both know where you live, so why don't we get out of here and go somewhere where we can relax and not be disturbed?"

"I'm game."

"I have just the spot. A good friend gave my kids a cabin just outside the Wisconsin Dells that is perfect for thinking through problems. Put some warm things in a bag and let's blow this joint."

Chapter 13

Truly relaxed for the first time in the last four months, Kayla lay across a finely woven, earth-toned Persian floor rug that adorned the wide-planked red oak hardwood flooring of the cabin's great room. Being relaxed and comfortable, she was free to allow her mind to roam back over the activities of the last three days and nights.

"Al was right, getting away from it all was just what I needed," Kayla thoughtfully concluded in her mind. She didn't even care that she had missed three days of work with no vacation time.

This being their last day at the cabin, they decided to hike to the town of Constance, which had existed for over 150 years two miles west of the cabin. In the town's general store they were told of a small eatery that resided in a turn-of-the-century log and stucco home-turned-restaurant.

The discussion about a restaurant that served great seafood just after completing a two-mile hike caused Kayla's mid-section to growl with desire. With the mention of the different items on the restaurant's menu, the pleasure that she was experiencing moved from her stomach to her face, expressing itself through her eyes and her generous smile.

"What do you think, Al? It would be my treat. After all, I have you to thank for the last few days."

"It's not like that, Kayla. I wanted to be here with you. Don't you understand that I want to be here with you? Don't you understand that I . . ."

Al was cut off by the sound of the 10:00 a.m. Tuesday-morning air raid siren that began its weekly ringing in a deafening tone from a fire station that stood just yards away from the store that they were in.

The siren stopped but the ringing sound in their ears made it seem like the siren was still ringing for at least a minute afterward. Able to hear herself talk again, Kayla wanted to know what was on Al's mind.

"What were you saying, Al?"

"I don't know. I lost my train of thought," Al lied to her after thinking better of what he was going to say before the siren interrupted him.

Dead Roots Wilting Flower

The walk back to the cabin had been slow and filled with lighthearted conversation. Over the course of the two-mile journey, they stopped many times to be in touch with nature.

One time they stopped to get a better look at three colts romping about in a fenced field. They watched the three horses playing peacefully under the soft late-morning sun. Noticing their audience, the largest horse, the coal black one with a blaze of white running the full length of his nose, slowly and with caution, approached the two of them. When the horse became more heedful, Al reached down and picked up a handful of hay that was lying outside the fence just beyond the reach of the horses and waived it at the observant animal.

Without any additional hesitation, the beautiful black work of art approached and began eating the hay that Al held out for him.

"How did you know how to make him come over to us?" Kayla questioned.

"You remember Dee, don't you?" Al inquired.

"Yeah, you know I do."

"Well he was a real country boy. We would go riding all the time. He taught me a little 'somethin somethin' about horses. Here, let me show you."

Al showed Kayla how to hold the hay out to the horses in a way that wouldn't lose a finger in the mouth of the heavy chewing horse. After seeing the attention that the black horse was getting, the other two horses — one brown and one gray — trotted over and began jockeying for the best position to get to the hay that was being offered.

Having no set time to do anything, the couple lingered around the horses for a while before continuing on their way. About a half-mile down the trail from the horses, they stopped alongside a slowly rambling, crystal clear stream. Subtle movement in the flow, caused by a cluster of small tadpoles fighting to swim upstream, against the slow-moving current, caught their attention.

The deep-green color of the baby frogs contrasted with the soft lake-blue of the stream water. The movements of the small aquatic creatures was slow, graceful, and seemingly made without a care in the world. No sooner did the thought go through her mind than a small trout appeared, poised to savor a tadpole lunch.

The sight of the small tadpoles, helpless against the larger fish, triggered a maternal feeling within Kayla. She knew that she had to protect the life inside of her at any cost. Her instinct for preservation rising to a heightened state, right then and there beside the stream, she decided that she would face James head-on when she returned to Chicago.

Kayla looked up into the surrounding woods from her kneeling position and was transported back in time again. Al, seeing what was happening, caught her slumping body. He laid her down by the water and rested her head on his jacket. He was no longer afraid of her spells and decided to just ride this one out quietly in the middle of the woods.

Dead Roots Wilting Flower

☙ ☙ ☙

John's hunting skill on many days would feed a family that would otherwise have gone hungry. A "boy man," his dogs, and his gun in the backwoods of Alabama was a lethal combination.

John liked hunting deep in a distant part of the woods that surrounded the small shanty town that everyone called "Whiskey Flats."

Champ and Captain would do their jobs and chase rabbits, squirrels, and coons well into the night. When night fell, and the nocturnal raccoon started its day, it was almost certain that Champ and Captain would have a coon holed up in the upper recesses of a tall oak tree.

"OK, guys, I hear you."

The barking of the dogs woke John out of a light slumber by the small fire.

"Good boys," John called out to the dogs in an encouraging voice. The barking of the dogs was enough to keep the raccoon perched in the tree as still as a tree limb would allow.

A flicker of John's flashlight revealed eyes that glistened and told him exactly where to aim his twelve-gauge shotgun. The thump on the forest floor told John that his aim had been true. Since the age of twelve, John had provided food for his fatherless family. Over the years, his shot had only gotten better.

As Champ and Captain were on their way to retrieve the coon, a second shot from beyond the light that the fire provided rang out. John turned suddenly as he heard the shot. On instinct, he was already reloading his twelve-gage.

The yelp from Champ was enough to let him know that the dog had been shot. Captain was by Champ's side as if standing guard. From where he stood John could see that Champ was down and that life was flowing from him.

"Hey, boy! You call that other dog back before I kill him too," a voice called from the darkness.

"Captain," John called in an urgent voice while still balancing his flashlight in one hand and his gun in the other, pointed forward, resting on his hip.

John sensed the situation, thanks to a lesson that his uncle had taught him on his first or second overnight stay in the woods behind Whiskey Flats.

"If someone comes into your camp uninvited you have to assume that the person doesn't mean you any good. It's either kill or be killed. Son, don't wait or ask any questions. Aim true, shoot first, and shoot to kill, son."

Now, facing the same situation that his uncle had described, for a split second John felt indecision coming over him until he could actually hear his uncle's voice; "Kill or be killed ... Aim true, shoot first and shoot to kill, son."

Now on automatic, John raised the flashlight a little higher, and again the glistening eyes told him where to aim.

"Get that light down bo..."

The voice was cut off as the shot echoed. John was void of all emotion. There was just the shot. Still on automatic, Champ and Bob Whiteside were put in the same shallow grave. A thought was given to making sure that Champ was on top in the grave. John's labor filling the grave was done with emotionless efficiency. The sun was up by the time he and Captain made it home with the coon.

꒓ ꒓ ꒓

Kayla recovered from her experience in Al's arms by the running water. That evening they decided to brake their routine of simple home-cooked meals and soul-searching conversation and committed to go out to the restaurant they had been told about.

꒓ ꒓ ꒓

Len needed to talk to the object of his desire. Four days ago when she had broken their date he started calling her two, sometimes three times a day. There was still no word from her. Part of his need was based on a genuine worry about Kayla. However, the biggest part of his need stemmed from his feeling that she was slipping away from him for a second time.

"What could've happened to her?" Len deliberated to himself while contemplating what he should do next.

"Maybe I should go to her house just to make sure she's OK," he continued to think already visualizing himself at her door. "I'll just ring her bell and ask her if she has been avoiding me."

Len's mind continued searching for a way to confront Kayla long after he was inside the Yellow cab and on his way to try and get her to see things his way. When no answer came to his mind about what to say to her and the cab already at the curb outside of her townhouse, Len undiscerningly decided to wing it.

Len mounted the townhouse's front stairs and knocked on the gray painted steel front door. The first knock yielded no answer. When the second knock yielded the same outcome, he began to look around the porch for a doorbell or other means of alarm. In his heart, he believed that Kayla was inside the townhouse.

Continuing his perusal of the porch area, Len noticed a tiny overstuffed mailbox. Seeing that mail had accumulated, he started to believe that she was not there hiding from him. With no reasonable alternatives in mind, Len had no choice but to leave.

Len slowly turned and began to descend the gray concrete stairs. Down the first two stairs, he looked right into the eyes of a floral delivery man who was making his way up.

"Good afternoon. I have a delivery for Ms. Kayla Wright."

"I'll take it. Ms. Wright isn't in right now, but I will make sure she gets it," Len replied in an authoritative voice.

"OK, just sign here, sir."

Len took the clipboard from the man and printed and wrote the name Ben Wright on line seven after Kayla's name and address. After handing the clipboard back to the driver, Len reached into his pocket and found five dollars to tip the driver.

Dead Roots Wilting Flower

"Thank you, Mr. Wright — Thank you."

Len smiled to himself, thinking about the power of a five dollar bill.

"You're welcome," he replied, with the vase and flowers already in his arms.

He watched the delivery van pull from the curb and slowly drive away. Sure that the van and its driver were gone, Len tore into the thin paper wrapping that shielded the flowers from his view. Once inside the paper, he could see twelve white long-stem roses surrounding two vivid red roses. The roses were intermixed with clusters of baby's breath and other assorted foliage.

Len understood that the assortment of flowers was meant to convey one's pure love to another. With that in mind, he launched into the arrangement with reckless abandon in search of a card from the sender. After his rough handling, the flowers would never be the same. Finding the card, he read it:

You've had my heart all the time
I just didn't know it
I love you — just me.

Len searched his mind.

"What man could Kayla know in Chicago?" Len asked himself.

His mind went back to the Green Dolphin and all the time that Kayla and Al had spent together there.

"That two-faced-back-stabbing asshole Al. He's supposed to be my friend. His ass is mine," flowed venomously from Len's mouth.

Chapter 14

Kayla continued daydreaming and relaxing while stretched out across the Oriental rug that rested on the great room floor. Al had a smooth but soulful jazz tune playing on the room's stereo at a low-easy sound level. She had never heard the song before and had no idea what the name of it was or whose sexy saxophone was putting goose bumps on her arms.

The nameless song reminded her of a slow, long night of sex. Sex, of any kind, was something that she had not experienced over the last three months.

"You would think that in my condition and with my issues sex would be the last thing I would want," she thought to herself, and then began fully embracing the amorous feeling that was growing inside of her.

She fashioned to herself that what she was just feeling a longing for some semblance of the good sex that had been a staple in her life before now. She also understood that the room's low lights, music, and the roaring fire dancing, spitting, and popping as it burned itself down, was adding to her unease. It was a restlessness that she did not want to control or get rid of. Sex was on her mind and, with limited options, she reconsidered Al.

Al, over the last three nights, had been too much the gentleman. Right now he was showering and getting ready for dinner out with her.

"I wonder if he knows," Kayla's thoughts continued.

"He's really not my type physically, but he does get something going inside of me," popped into her mind, causing her to turn her head toward the bathroom door.

From her vantage point on the floor, Kayla could see that the bath's door was slightly ajar and that colorless rays of light were escaping through its left and right jambs.

"One look won't hurt," she assured herself.

She quietly rose to her feet and tiptoed over to the hinge side of the bathroom door. Staying as quiet as possible, she peered through the sliver of space between the door and the door jamb. Undetected, she watched Al as he unwrapped a blue terrycloth towel from around his waist and drew it vigorously across his chocolate-colored back.

Dead Roots Wilting Flower

She could see the towel picking up tiny droplets of water that looked as if they were enjoying clinging to a man's skin. Exploring his broad back, with her eyes she followed his torso down to a trim waist. His back gave way to two well-defined cheeks that flexed and called her name every time he moved.

He possessed an ass that protruded gracefully from the small of his back and proceeded down to and cupped his thighs. It formed the perfect little half bubble that glistened under the bathroom lights due to the remaining moisture that was deposited there.

"Stealing a look at a man. How low have I fallen?" Kayla asked herself just as Al turned around, revealing another side of himself to her.

Al was brown and she always went for men that were much lighter. However, right now she found herself enjoying the look of this well-toned man. Now, offering a side view to her, she saw a low-hanging not circumcised ray of flesh extending from a washboard stomach and bush of perfectly lying black hair.

Her eyes did not move from their job of inspecting every inch of everything that she could see. Her head moved up and down the length of his body in a slow but constant motion.

He dragged the towel between his muscular legs, taking care to lift and move his dick and cheeks out of the way of the towel's rubbing action. On automatic, he took himself in his hand, pinched back his foreskin, and dried the hidden area.

At this precise moment, she would have given anything to be that blue terrycloth towel absorbing his essence. Oh, just to be that cloth exploring all of the places that were reserved for her alone.

Without any warning, Al reached over and pushed closed the door to the bathroom completely. Her imagination remained open, along with her desire to see more and be held and fulfilled.

Al was surprised that he was ready to go to dinner before Kayla was ready. For the last three days, he had never been ready to go anywhere before her. In fact, he was notoriously known for being a slow dresser. It wasn't something that he did on purpose; it just happened that way.

For Al, showering, shaving, filing his nails, combing his hair, brushing his teeth, etc., were all done in a meticulous manner, taking care not to miss any detail. He considered the time spent on these activities his time. It was time that was not divided among other things like work, friends, and so on. During this time, the clock stopped ticking for him and the entire world revolved only around him. It was a special time for him.

Ready first. This was one for the books. The strangeness of being first was emphasized by a few small things that had changed in the great room of the cabin since he had been there last, about forty-five minutes before. Most noticeable were the three tall raspberry-scented candles flickering in the room, providing soft light in areas not illuminated by the glow cast from the fireplace. There also was the music of Pat Metheny playing in the background. It wasn't the music itself that was strange to him. It was the higher volume that seemed unusual.

Al liked his music at a volume that didn't overpower. Music for him was played at an understated volume. He kept it at a volume that allowed the listener to fully function at whatever else they might be doing and still be soothed. The volume of the music indeed had been raised.

Yes, there was something truly in the air; it was unmistakable. Even the tiny little hairs that ran their way from the base of his neck down to and trailing off at the center of his shoulder blades were standing on end and tingling.

Al's thoughts were interrupted by Kayla's entrance.

"Al, would you be too upset if we didn't go tonight?" Kayla asked, walking from the back bedroom to the great room where Al was still trying to gain his bearings.

"It's your night. It's up to you."

"Let's order a pizza for delivery. OK?"

Kayla was right in front of him and Al noticed that she was not dressed. She had on a shear, full-length, deep blue robe that allowed her erect nipples to show off.

After ordering pizza, Kayla sat on the floor using, the back of the couch as a backrest. She began to reveal her intentions.

"I thought it would be nice just the two of us tonight."

Her eyes never left Al's face in their pursuit of trying to read his reactions. Wanting to make her point clear, she allowed her bare leg and lower thigh to peak out of the slit in the robe. Kayla knew that her legs were still her best asset.

"I like what you like. You should know that by now." Al gave in to what was in the air.

"I think I do."

Kayla moved across the floor over to where Al was sitting in an easy chair looking at her with an inquisitive expression. Without a word, now directly in front him, she leaned her head on his knee, closed her eyes, and began to dream.

Al instinctively reached down and began stroking her hair.

"I don't want to hurt anyone any more," Al said in a low soft voice that was barely audible.

"I'm a big girl. I know what I want. You're not responsible for my feelings."

Remembering the adage that less is sometimes more, Al didn't say a word. He had what he wanted: she was ready to give herself to him. There were no words that could describe how he was feeling.

Before long they both were in a chair holding each other and sharing long, deep kisses that seemed to last for hours. Kayla, wanting to feel everything that she had seen earlier that evening, began rubbing over every part of his body. Her angle was bad, and she knew that sitting in a chair was not going to get her what she wanted.

"Come on, let's lie in front of the fire," she suggested into Al's ear.

For the longest while they searched each other's bodies. Everything was revealed.

"Is this what I think it is?" Al asked as his fingers paused, from their prior roaming, at the base of her stomach.

"Well that depends. What do you think it is?"

"Come on, Kayla," Al said while licking her stomach and twirling his tongue in her navel. "It's showing, and besides, your chest is tender."

Kayla began wrapping her robe around her now naked body.

"Oh no you don't. I've waited too long to be right here."

Al reached out and grabbed her around her waist, whispering, "I want to love you any way you are. Kayla, as strange as it sounds, it doesn't matter to me. Can I have tonight?"

"I know I started this but it is not a good idea. You know. . ."

Al did not want to hear what she was saying so he cut her off with, "Remember how we started this. We'll take this one step at a time. One day at a time."

Al continued to ignore her reservations and the look on her face and went back to the adage of less being more. He should have never brought up what he saw. To remedy things, he decided to go for broke. Within minutes, his tongue was fully extended in and out of her pussy. Softly first, followed by soft bites and licking as if she were an ice cream cone. Her deep moan told all.

The first ringing sound from the doorbell was mistaken as being a part of the background music. The second ring followed by a hard knock was beyond mistake. Someone was at the cabin door.

"We forgot the pizza!" Al remembered out loud.

Al reached the door completely in the buff. Unashamed, he opened the door and handed the delivery man a twenty and told him to keep the change.

Kayla, from her position in front of the fireplace, was completely taken at how unashamed of his body Al was. There was no shame in how he was hanging, and she just lay there enjoying him swing back and forth as he fetched plates, a bottle of Shiraz wine, and two glasses.

Kayla didn't want any pizza. When Al came within reach, she reached up, grabbed him, and tugged him directly into her mouth.

She didn't want him to come so she brought him to a high point with her hands and mouth and then stopped to let him calm down a bit. Before long, she started again. Her actions went off and on for over twenty minutes until she decided that she wanted some wine with him. In her condition she couldn't drink it so she decided to pour it on his monster so she could taste him and the wine together.

Al licked, sucked, nibbled, and explored the set of lips that still allowed her to tell him just how good he was making her feel. They were working up to intercourse, but they already knew each other more intimately than couples who had already had sex.

The heavy petting was intermixed with Al playing music for her, and she listened and enjoyed it and him.

"Hold on! What's that?" Al asked.

He rose from his position on the floor and turned down the stereo. His pager was vibrating in the pocket of his pants resting on the floor. He couldn't ignore it.

Cell phone in hand, Al dialed his answering machine and listened in horror. This night was over and within the hour they were speeding south toward Chicago.

Chapter 15

Having been in Chicago for almost four full days, James still had not seen Kayla. In his mind, he was running out of options. When he first arrived, he did talk to her for a few minutes and she promised to call him back. Since then he had not heard from her.

In a move to try and get her attention, he had sent her fourteen roses — two red and a dozen white. He hoped that the flowers would spur a reply from her. At least a thank you. Each day, he found himself calling her four or five times but each time, to his dismay, there was no answer. In his hotel room, his hopes, desires, and love went unanswered.

Having grown tired of the same four walls staring back at him for the last four days as he waited for Kayla's call, he decided to go downstairs and have dinner for a change. Room service had been the order of the day for the last three days. "What sense did it make to stay at a five-star hotel like the Westin and not enjoy it a little?" He thought to himself.

Entering the restaurant off of the main lobby and looking around, he quickly decided to have dinner at the bar where he could read the paper, watch Sports Center, and have a drink.

"Hello, can I order dinner here at the bar?" James inquired of a late-twenties-something white bartender.

"Of course. Just pull up a stool and I'll be right with you."

The bartender was dressed completely in black except for a white apron neatly tied around a thickening waist. A few minutes later the waiter returned with an oversized white napkin, silver, salt and pepper shakers, and a menu. Without saying a word, he neatly arranged the items on the bar in front of James.

"Thank you, Richard," James offered after reading the bartender's name on his name tag.

"You're welcome. Can I get you something from the bar while you're looking over the menu?" Richard asked, pleased that his patron took the time to note his name.

"Yeah. I'll have a Becks Dark if you have one."

"Did you notice that we have Becks Dark on tap?" Richard offered.

Dead Roots Wilting Flower

"No, I didn't; thanks. I'll have a pint from the tap."

"Great," Richard replied, with a revealing lisp in his voice.

As Richard walked away to draw the beer from the tap at the other end of the bar, he glanced over his shoulder and gave James a wicked smile. James was used to this type of come-on from men and paid it very little attention.

The Wednesday night crowd in the bar was very slow, and James felt very comfortable settling in and lounging there. Six beers, an order of calamari, and a chicken Caesar salad went well with the "USA Today" and the Bulls/Lakers game playing on the three barroom televisions.

All through the night, Richard made sure that James was well taken care of. The attention came with a price. The more Richard served James, the more friendly he became with his comments and conversation.

"How was your meal?"

"Uh, I mean. It was great," James answered.

"What did you say your name was?"

"Sam — Sam Smith," James replied.

"Well Sam, do you see anything else that you want?" Richard inquired with a hopeful anticipation while holding his arms open in an inviting manner.

James understood where Richard was going with his question.

"I don't know," James replied with a flirtatious pause before continuing, "Let me see your dessert menu."

Over the years James' lack of sensitivity to being propositioned often paid dividends. It wasn't uncommon for him to be given something on the house by allowing these types of advances to go unchecked even when they were unwanted. The norm was half off at clothing stores and free food at restaurants. He knew how and when to flaunt his looks and make them pay off for him. Most times, the advances were unwanted, but he let them continue for the thrill of getting something for free.

The bar conversation between Richard and James continued for a short while. Hearing Richard's continued innuendoes, James reassured himself often during the exchange that he himself wasn't gay. However, he felt good being wanted by a man.

Six-working-on-seven beers were helping to confuse the feelings pounding in his head. The feelings were having their way with him. James first felt the feeling in high school and decided on a little experimentation. One thing, over the years, led to another and somehow his diverse sexual appetite had gotten him into his present torn-between-love-and-thrill situation.

"What brings you to Chicago, Sam?" Richard wanted to know.

"My baby moved here and I'm looking for her."

"Well, Chicago is a big city. Do you need some help finding love tonight?" Richard asked optimistically.

James' current state of mind was very stressed. It was that stress that allowed him to think about the physical release that was being offered to him.

"Sure, what the hell. When you get off of work, I'm in room 17610. You can stop by. OK?"

James gave in to wanting something but not wanting it at the same time. He took out his wallet to pay for his meal and asked, "What's my tab?"

"Oh, it's on the house tonight. I'll see you about one," Richard informed him.

James reached his room and noticed the time. It was already five minutes to twelve. "Just enough time to shower and wash my ass," he thought to himself.

Continuing into the room, James noticed that the message light on the phone was blinking. Beyond himself with anticipation, he quickly advanced to the bed, sat down, and picked up the phone to retrieve his messages.

"Nine O Seven p.m.," the mechanical voice on the answering machine announced.

"James, it's Bobby checking on you. I don't know what I did to make you go all the way to Chicago. Anyway, call me when you get a chance. Bye."

James was disappointed that it was his New York issue following him to Chicago and not Kayla on the phone. The disappointment turned into anticipation when the mechanical voice returned to announce another received call.

"Ten Eleven p.m," the mechanical phone voice rang out into James' ear.

"OK, where are you? This is Kayla calling you back like I said I would. Sorry it took so long but I needed to get my thoughts together. Uh, I'll give you a call first thing in the morning at about eight o'clock. Maybe we can do breakfast? Talk to you then."

James was so excited to hear from Kayla that he remained seated on the bed holding the phone to his ear for a few seconds as if he were in a trance. Waking from his trance-like state, he hit the replay button and listened to Kayla's message a second time trying, to pick up the little nuances in her voice as she spoke. He listened intently trying to discern if she were still mad at him or if she was looking forward to seeing him again. Over the next few moments, Al lingered on the edge of the bed just thinking about Kayla.

James finally put the phone back on its cradle and took note that time was slipping away. It was almost twelve thirty. With Kayla's call taking up all of his mental energy, he lost all desire for the candy cane that was coming to his room. Feeling like he was making headway and his trip to Chicago was a good move after all, he lingered a second or two longer, sitting on the bed thinking about what he was going to do.

"Shit! What's done is done, I guess," he said out loud to himself as he headed for the bathroom and a hot shower.

℈ ℈ ℈

Kayla was true to her word. She called James at eight sharp. Her plan was to meet with him by nine and arrive at work by ten thirty.

"Hello," James answered the phone between its first and second rings.

"OK, James you have one hour before I get there. Be ready. I don't have a lot of time; I have to go to work."

"Kayla, I'm just waking up."

"Hey, it's the early bird that gets the worm. If you want, we can put this off unti..."

Not wanting to lose her into the depths of Chicago again, James cut her off by saying, "OK, what time will you be here?"

"I'll be there by nine. You need to be ready so I don't have to be any later to work than I need to be."

"I've been ready for five days," James sourly retorted, now awake and thinking.

"Whatever, James. Nine o'clock, OK? Bye."

James put the phone down and looked over to the other side of the bed and sighed.

"Hey, buddy. You've got to get up. I don't have much time," James called to his guest.

Richard also was awakened by the ring of the phone. Wanting to hear the conversation, he lay still on the bed pretending to be asleep as the exchange between James and the caller moved forward. He had a clue who it was on the other side of the conversation and was a little upset that a woman was giving James a hard time. His outrage was especially high since he was right there to make everything all right for James.

Being kicked out of a lover's bed, like he had a reason to be, Richard felt a little insulted. Not being one to take things lying down, he rose and sprang into action. Dressing quickly, he made a point of not putting on his t-shirt and standard white, too small for James' protruding ethnic butt, underwear. Richard hid his t-shirt and underwear calling card under the sheet at the foot of the bed.

"OK, buddy, I'll be here a few more days. Why don't you stay in touch?" James offered, knowing full well that he had no intentions of ever going there again.

It wasn't that the way Richard held and stroked his dick didn't turn him on. Surely, it wasn't that Richard licked his dick like it was a Butterfinger, causing him to ejaculate almost instantaneously. It was the fact that James had someone else on his mind that left no room for these luxuries.

"It was fun. I left my number by the phone. Maybe we can finish what we started," Richard said, clearly letting his girlish manner come into full effect.

"James, I'm downstairs," Kayla spoke into the lobby phone.

"Come on up. The room number is 17610."

"OK. Bye."

Heavy with expectation, James unlocked the room door and waited in the hallway outside. His heart fluttered when he saw her approaching. She was too busy looking at the room numbers on the doors, making sure that she was headed in the right direction, to notice him as she approached. As seconds passed, James could feel the ponderous beating of his heart. When she finally did see him, to James' dismay, her walk sped up toward him and he was forced to stop admiring her from afar and face what lay ahead.

"Hey, baby; you look good," James said to Kayla walking toward her with his arms wide open for what he hoped would be a reconciling hug.

As if she didn't see him, Kayla walked past him with only a small nod of her head. Undaunted by her actions, James followed behind her and reached over her shoulder to open the door to the room for her. He took his time pushing open the door, taking the opportunity to press his body close to hers while smelling her essence.

Kayla paid no attention to James' crass act and acted as if she didn't feel his body touching hers. As soon as she was able, she entered the room and took a seat in a comfortable high-backed chair located near the room's balcony windows.

After a moment, Kayla turned up her nose and asked, "What's that smell, James?"

The room contained the lingering smell of the past night's activities. Having been in the room all night, James' sense of smell was not sensitive to the pungent odor.

"I don't know. I don't smell anything," James responded.

Not wanting to linger on something unimportant in the little time that she had, Kayla switched the subject to the main issue.

"Well, James, I'm here. It's your dime, so what's on your mind? I personally thought that you said everything you needed to say a few months back at the restaurant."

"I didn't tell you that I loved you that day."

"James, that love wasn't enough to keep you from someone else's arms or from crushing me, was it? No, James, that tired 'I love you' shit is not enough for me anymore."

Kayla was torn on the inside, knowing that their future was hanging in the balance.

He knows what he is doing. Knowing that I was coming by, he put on those tight coach's shorts to show off the full length of his thing, Kayla speculated to herself.

Needing to change her train of thought, she rose from the chair and out of the line of sight of his crotch and walked toward the balcony windows.

"Look, love wasn't enough in New York. What makes you think that it is now?" she inquired again.

Needing to be close, James walked over to her and took her hand.

"Please, don't do this to us. I'll do anything to make things right between us. Baby, I love you so much," he pleaded.

"Don't you understand how deeply you hurt me? Before this conversation goes any further, there's something that you need to know. James, I'm..."

Before she could finish her sentence, the door to the room eased open and a voice called in.

Dead Roots Wilting Flower

"Excuse me. Hello. Hi Sam! Sorry for barging in but I forgot my..." Richard was cut off mid-sentence.

James, nervous and agitated, looking at Kayla and then back at Richard huffed, "Now is not a good time. Can you come back later?"

"I just want to pick up my undershirt and panties, girlfriend. I've got to have something to put back on." Richard was making his sexuality known by the inflection of his voice.

"James, who is this man?" Kayla asked in a slow, measured voice.

"So, James is your real name. It does fit you," Richard said while hungrily looking James up and down before he moved with a switch to the bed to retrieve his personal items from under the sheets.

Ignoring Kayla's question and Richard's comment, James started moving toward Richard with anger in his eyes.

Seeing James, Richard quickly headed toward the room door yelling out, "I'll give you some more of what I gave you last night if you need it when you finish with her, baby!"

Following him outside the room, James lost control of himself and slammed his fist into Richard's stomach.

"Mother fucker, don't you know I'll kill you?" James said, with the sound of death in his voice.

The only thing that saved James from himself was remembering the emergency that he still had in his room.

I have to get back in the room and explain. His thoughts raced.

"This isn't over, you bitch. I'm going to make sure you never do this to anyone else in this hotel," James stated. Before he walked back into the room, he planted a departing knee to Richard's groin.

Walking through the doorway, James immediately looked deep within Kayla's face and into her eyes to try and read her mind and figure out what he had to do to win her back.

Oh my GOD! Kayla exclaimed inside her head. *OK, girl, calm down. There has to be a logical explanation,* she continued thinking to herself.

She was slowly sorting through the scene she had just witnessed. One at a time, she was easing off of her the ton of bricks that had made its way onto her mind, holding her there unable to move from her standing spot at the room's balcony windows. She was startled by the sound of James' voice.

"Sorry about that interruption. Where were we?"

Still falling out of her trance-like state, her mind willed her to say, "No! Hell, no! You're not going to play me like nothing just happened, are you?"

After trying to say it out loud, her ears informed her that nothing had come out of her mouth.

"Kayla, are you all right," James asked in a sincere voice that would have been calming in any other situation.

Dead Roots Wilting Flower

Her mouth was still very dry but she was finally able to form words through it.

"No, James! I'm not all right! What do you think; you act like I wasn't even here! Like I didn't see that — that thing that was in here."

"No, it's not like that, baby."

"Baby? Did you just call me baby? James are you gay?"

"No," James heaved out of his mouth, not knowing what else to say.

After a brief pause in which Kayla didn't take her questioning eyes off of him, he offered, "It was something that just...happened."

"So you mean to tell me that you just happened to fall into bed with a man?"

"It's not like that, Kayla. It was just that. . ."

"I don't want to know! All I need to know is when did this start happening?"

"Look at it this way. . ."

"Damn it! Please just answer my question." Kayla was trying to hold herself together.

"It's been happening on and off for awhile."

"Before and during the time you were seeing me?"

"Yeah. I mean . . ."

"James, how in the hell could you do this to me. What if... no I can't even think about it. I have to go."

"Kayla, wait!"

Before the words were out of his mouth, Kayla was out the door and on her way down the hall. James caught up with her at the elevator.

"Look, girl, I love you. Doesn't that mean anything to you?"

"No, right now James, it doesn't. I'm not going to deal with this right now. I'm just not," she informed him and re-pushed the down arrow for the elevator again, hoping that it would speed its arrival.

"Will you at least call me later after you have calmed down?"

The look on her face gave him his answer and made him plead more.

"It doesn't have to be today. What about tomorrow or the next day," he cried with his voice.

The elevator arrived, forcing James to block the metal doorway with his body and urge her with his body language.

Kayla, needing this to be over, replied, "OK, OK — whatever you want James."

"Thank you. I'll make all of this up to you. Thank you."

James moved out of the way of the elevator. "You won't be sorry," was shouted through the closing elevator door.

Chapter 16

"OK. I think I got it," Tracie said to Kayla as if a light bulb just lit inside of her head. "So you used to love James, who let you down, got you pregnant, now is gay, and doesn't know that you may bring a child of his into this world. Do I have that part right, girl?"

"Yes, and it sounds worse when you say it like that," Kayla complained.

"Now there's Len who was your man before James, who won't leave you alone, and is good friends with Al," Tracie continued, to confirm her understanding of the weave of events that her new friend had lain on her.

"You have it right so far."

"Lastly, there's my man Al, who has become your friend, knows that you're pregnant, you're starting to have feelings for him, but you're afraid you're just rebounding."

If Kayla had been paying closer attention to Tracie, she would have noticed the change in her voice and manner when she started talking about Al. As it was, Kayla just answered her.

"Yes, Al is just an innocent bystander in all of this."

"Now remember, Kayla, you called me over for advice. Right? Because I'm not the kind of girl that bites her tongue," Tracie warned.

"No. I want to know what you think."

"Well if it were me, I wouldn't say anything to any of them. First off, Len sounds like he needs to get a life and get over it. My mama told me, when I asked her why she never took my daddy back, to never go backward girl. I've lived by that advice. Once I kick them to the curb, they stay down there and there ain't no coming back."

Tracie stopped talking long enough to take a long drag of the Miller Genuine Draft beer that she was drinking. It was her fourth one, and the beer was starting to loosen up her speech.

Tracie wiped some lingering beer from her lips with the back of her hand and continued.

"You've got to confront a man like Len. It's a testosterone thing. They all want what they can't have, and he's not going to stop trying to get it until you tell him definitively to leave you the hell alone."

"I know you're right because every time I try to talk to him he only hears what he wants to hear," Kayla told

Tracie, while thinking back over her recent encounters with Len.

"Girl, do you want me to get rid of him for you? Don't forget that I work for UPS; that's just like the Post Office. He better stay out of your face or I might go postal on him," Tracie said in a way that one could not tell if she were joking or serious.

Just to be on the safe side, Kayla replied, "No. It's my issue. I'll take care of it."

"So we got him taken care of; let's get to James. He's the real fucker here."

"I have to at least tell him that he's going to be a father."

"Father!" Tracie shouted, pushing out of her mouth and down the side of her chin a drop of beer that she had just sipped. "It takes more than what he's done to be called a father. Right now all he has done is plant a seed."

The drop of beer that was on Tracie's face continued a slow descent down her chin while the look on Kayla's face revealed that Tracie was not getting through to her. Seeing Kayla's indecision and feeling the moisture on her chin, Tracie took a different approach. She removed the moisture from her chin with her index finger and placed her finger in her mouth.

Almost not getting her finger out of her mouth in time to talk, Tracie became loud and said, "Girl, from what you have told me about him and his lifestyle, do you even want him in your child's and your lives?"

"I don't know. This is all new to me. Damn, damn, damn. Why me?"

"Look. If the test comes back positive, and he wants you to still keep the baby, then what? You've already told me you didn't want any pressure about what to do. Girl, don't give no man, least of all that one, that kind of power in your life. Don't tell that lying sack of shit nothing."

"I can't face him right now anyway. If I did I don't know what I might do."

"Good, then it's settled. You're not going to talk to him. At least not now. You have time. Wait for the results and then we can figure it out from there," Tracie asserted.

The room was silent for a few minutes while Tracie visited the bathroom for the third time since she had been at Kayla's townhouse. While in the bathroom, Tracie washed her hands again. Since coming to Kayla's house, she didn't feel that she could get her hands clean enough.

Tracie returned from the bathroom and continued. "What about Al?" The question was asked rhetorically since she knew that she wanted to control this situation.

Needing an answer, Tracie continued, "You haven't slept with him have you?"

"No! We're just friends," Kayla lied, remembering that Tracie and Al were co-workers, and if something like this were to get out in the workplace it could be devastating.

Tracie breathed a sigh of relief, then continued. "Good. Then I see no reason to get him involved at all. OK? He's a good guy. Why get him involved in all of this?"

Kayla was quiet and without an answer. Of all people, including Tracie, she wanted to talk to Al. Knowing that he was already involved, she decided within herself that Tracie was probably right. She needed to keep everyone out of it for now.

"You're right, Tracie. I don't need to talk to anyone else right now," Kayla said in a sad, low voice.

"When we go down there tomorrow, wear something comfortable. When I went last year, they had me down there all morning."

"Will I have to give them my real name?" Kayla asked.

"No. They'll assign you a number, then make you sit through a boring movie on all of the sexually transmitted diseases that are out there now. After that, there's a presentation on birth control and then another movie on intimacy. I guess since they're giving you a free service, they feel that they can take up all of your day."

"Maybe most of the people coming into the Board of Health are younger and need to know the information," Kayla rationalized.

"Maybe. After all of that you finally pee into a cup and give them some blood. They tell you to call them in a few days and give them your number. When I called they told me that I was fine, and that was it."

"I shouldn't have to go through this at all. Who would have thought that James would do something like that. Just thinking about it makes my skin crawl."

Kayla was close to tears as she reflected on the bomb that had been dropped on her today.

"I think everyone should know. So just look at it as a good thing. I'ma go to the bathroom to wash my hands then get out of here girl."

ʓ ʓ ʓ

After taking a full, deep breath of fresh air once outside of Kayla's townhouse, Tracie felt better.

"That's more like it," Tracie said to herself, walking to her car.

Tracie was safely in her car and on her way to the West Side via the Eisenhower Expressway. She looked at the clock on the car's dashboard and noticed that it was ten-thirty. In the next instant, she decided that before she drove too far west, she should call Al to see if he needed anything.

"Hey, Al. Where have you been? I've tried to call you the last few days ... Oh. How was it? ... Did you go alone? ... Being way up there in the woods with all that fresh air must have made you a little randy, huh ... So with your big day and all tomorrow, I guess you don't want any company? ... Well I'ma just go on home then. See you at work. Bye."

The rest of Tracie's ride home was made in silence. She didn't feel the need for the radio to keep her company; her mind was on how to get what she wanted.

Chapter 17

The page that Al had received while in Wisconsin was about O'ne. It hit Al hard to find out that O'ne had had an accident. While eating dinner, the message said, she fell out of her high chair. Both her grandmother and grandfather said that they had only taken their eyes off of her for a second.

Everyone was relieved that O'ne's fall resulted only in a bad head bruise on her head and not a skull fracture which was the message that was left on Al's answering machine. However, the emergency room nurse noticed, without comment to the Clarks, that their age and frailty would not allow them to properly care for a two-year-old rambunctious child. Her observations mandated that she take action.

The nurse asked the grandparents if they were the sole guardians of O'ne. Their half truthful reply of "yes" betrayed them.

Fearing for the child's safety, the nurse asked the attending physician to admit O'ne to the hospital for the night. In view of the late hour, the bruise, and the grandparents' finally admitting that the child had slipped out of her grandmother's hands while she was being removed from her high chair, it didn't take much to convince the doctor.

Not knowing that O'ne had a caring father, the nurse took the extra step of calling the Department of Children and Family Services to inform them of the child's injuries and how they had happened. The nurse's observation that the grandparents lacked the physical mobility to care for a young child was given weight by the social service intake personnel.

3 3 3

Al listened intently to Attorney Irene Holt as she outlined her thoughts relative to him gaining custody of his daughter while they waited for court to begin. After firing his last attorney, Al had interviewed four different lawyers before choosing Attorney Holt. Al chose her because, she possessed over thirty years of experience handling these types of cases and came recommended by two different Chicago area bar associations. It was also very important that she communicated with him in a manner that he was comfortable with. There was none of the condescending, "Don't worry, I'll handle it," conversation from her. She took the time to explain everything that she was doing and why she was doing it.

Al was also impressed with her soft-spoken confidence. It seemed that a common trait among lawyers was over-the-top confidence. She was the first one to set out all of the ways that he could be unsuccessful in his desire to raise his child as well as all of the ways that he could be successful.

With her, there was a unified plan that included bringing in specialists as required. She also said up front that if Al wasn't ready to spend upward of fifty thousand dollars in addition to what he had already spent, it might be a good idea to try and settle the case instead of fighting the grandparents. She was also adamant, and made sure Al understood, that even after spending that kind of money, there were no guarantees.

Today, she explained to Al, her thoughts revolved around an emergency motion. Attorney Holt was sure that the Judge would hear the motion because it spoke to the basic welfare of O'ne

Again, Al was going into a courtroom filled with hope. Before the judge were Attorney Holt, the grandparents' attorney, and a heavyset African American woman whom Al had never seen before.

"Your honor this is *In re* the matter of O'ne Gold vs. Albert Gold. Today we're here before you with Mr. Gold's emergency motion asking you to enter an order for the immediate surrender of possession of the minor child to her natural father, Mr. Gold," Attorney Holt recited in a tone that sounded more like she was singing a song than talking.

"Counsel, I have taken the opportunity to read your pleadings," the Judge informed her. "Before we move to the merits of the allegations in your motion, I want to know who I have before me today," Judge Nixon requested.

"Good morning, your honor. Bernie Leverwitz on behalf of the maternal grandparents, Mr. and Mrs. Clark," the grandparents' attorney advised.

"Your honor, Birdie Mae Jordan from the Department of Children and Family Services."

The white woman judge, who looked to be in her late fifties, was busy making notes in her log as the people before her spoke. Once finished writing, she looked up and began.

"Now that we have the introductions out of the way, I think that we have one more bit of housekeeping to do. Ms. Holt, I see that Mr. Goldman still has his 'appearance' on file as the attorney of record for Mr. Gold. I don't see an 'appearance' on file for you," the judge inquired.

It was clear that the judge had done her homework on this case and was going to be methodical and by the book.

"I'm sorry, your honor, I thought that my substitute appearance would have made it into the file by now,"

Dead Roots Wilting Flower

Attorney Holt offered, as she searched her file folder for the piece of paper that she needed.

Finding the paper, Attorney Holt continued. "We filed our appearance almost two weeks ago, your honor," she said with confidence and handed the "appearance" to the judge.

"Mr. Leverwitz, do you have any reply to the motion? It seems that the child was hurt while in your clients' care," the judge said all the while coldly looking at him.

"Yes, your honor, I am aware of the child being brought to the hospital, but I fail to see how this should result in tearing this child from the only home she knows. Additionally, now that DCFS is involved, I don't think that we have an emergency on our hands today."

Attorney Holt's voice lowered an octave, and she raised its volume for the argument that lay ahead.

"Your honor, we have a little girl that hospital personnel were afraid to release to the care of the grandparents for reasons that we have outlined in our motion. All we ask is that you give Mr. Gold permission to go get his child from the hospital. To be able to comfort his child," Attorney Holt said in a slow, measured tone that exhibited confidence.

The judge raised her brow as if asking a question, then began, "I reviewed the file and I don't find the required documentation that would allow me to release this child to Mr. Gold. I can't take her out of a bad situation and put her into what might be a worse one. I know that you just came into this case, Ms. Holt, but there are no home studies and no evaluations in the file. My hands are tied."

The judge was covering her back on this day. It was clear to everyone in the courtroom but Al that O'ne would not be coming home with him today.

"Your honor, what would you have us do? Leave the child at the hospital or place her back in the same situation that she was in?" Attorney Holt asked these questions knowing what the judge would do next.

"I need to hear from Ms. Jordan," the judge requested.

"In light of the circumstances as we know them, as of this morning we have taken the child into DCFS custody," said Birdie Mae Jordan.

"What," Al shouted from where he was seated. "I can take care of my child."

"Ms. Holt, you are going to get your client under control and have him refrain from this type of outburst," the judge demanded.

"Your honor, can I have a moment with my client?"

"Yes, you do that. Do that. The court will stand in recess for ten minutes," the judge said, emphasizing her unhappiness with Al's actions by slamming her hand on the bench.

Attorney Holt caught up with Al in the back of the courtroom.

"Al, you have to control yourself! This is a courtroom; you are not out in the streets. Remember, it didn't take one day for this mess to get this bad. You have to believe in me at least through this court appearance."

"I know. I just lost it. But Attorney Holt, what is a child of mine doing in DCFS's hands?"

"It's not going to be that bad. You will be able to see her."

"Anything could happen to her there."

"OK. Here's what we're going to do. First you must understand that what is happening here today was out of our control before we even stepped into the courtroom. Right now, the judge has all of the cards. However, it's times like these when we must do our best work. What we need to do is find out what's on the judge's mind and then conform ourselves as best as possible to it."

"How long is this going to take?" Al questioned.

"Right now, I don't know. I won't leave this courtroom today until I have as much information as possible, and you know that I will try to make things happen as quickly as possible."

"I'm with you, Attorney Holt," Al said halfheartedly.

She reached out and took Al's chin in her hands, forcing him to look directly at her.

"I really need to know if you're with me," she demanded, with just the right blend of compassion and strength.

"Yes, I'm with you," he said, with a little more heart this time.

"No more outbursts!"

Al nodded in the affirmative and Attorney Holt returned to the front of the courtroom to wait for the judge to return. During the wait, she approached the judge's clerk.

"You look good. When did you have the baby?"

"Thanks, she's two months now," the clerk replied with a big smile.

"How did you drop the weight so fast?"

"You know a baby keeps you busy."

"Do you have a snapshot of her?"

The clerk pointed to a color photo of a cute baby girl crudely taped to the side of the filing cabinet that stood next to the clerk's desk.

"She is adorable . . . "

Just then, the judge returned to the courtroom, and the respective attorneys approached the bench.

Without asking anything else from the three people in front of her, the judge began ruling.

"I'm ordering Supportive Services to perform a home study on an expedited basis of the father's and the grandparents' homes. Until the results of the home studies are returned, I see no reason to remove the child from her current placement with the Department of Children and Family Services. I will see all parties here with their attorneys, including the child, in thirty days. Ms. Holt will you draw up that order?"

"Yes, your honor."

After writing the order and showing it to Attorney Leverwitz, Attorney Holt gave it to the clerk to have the judge sign it. While standing in front of the clerk, she made a mental note to herself to pick up an inexpensive frame for the photo of the clerk's baby. Now her work was done for the day.

ʒ ʒ ʒ

Dr. King and Al were finishing up their session and Al felt good.

Since there were a few minutes left in their hour appointment, as an aside, Dr. King asked Al about Terow.

"Are you still having disturbing thoughts about your ex-girlfriend?"

Al began to reply, "I still ..."

ʒ ʒ ʒ

"Te what are you doing here?" Al asked in amazement.

Over the last few months, Al had begun to embrace Terow coming to him. This time it was as if she were actually sitting across from him.

"Al, I've been close to you and O'ne ever since I died," Terow explained.

Still not understanding, Al replied with, "Oh," and continued to try to figure out her presence.

"I know that our time is short, so I want to get right to the point. Al you have to accept Jesus as your savior or you are going to wind up just like me," Terow warned in a serious tone. "I've been searching for someone to seek forgiveness for me since I died."

"What are you talking about, Te? I don't understand," Al questioned.

Terow continued her warning, "We don't have a whole lot of time. Remember to take some time out and make sure your life is in order. You have to or you're going to regret it."

Watching her time Terow continued. "Until you get your life right your roots are dead. You need roots. The roots that only accepting Jesus as your personal savior can provide."

"OK. Consider it done," Al promised.

"It's important, Al. I can't tell you how important it really is."

There was a moment of silence between them. The silence revived Al and left him feeling better than he had before Terow came to him.

"You're doing a good job with O'ne. I am proud of the way that you have stepped up to the plate and are fighting for her. I always knew that you would be her knight."

"I'm trying, Te, but it's sometimes hard to know what the right thing to do is. Everyone has feelings and someone is always getting theirs hurt," Al explained.

"Follow your heart, Al. Follow your heart and everything will be OK."

"I will."

"You better go back before you have to stay," Terow cautioned.

"Before I go, I want you to know that I am sorry for not being there for you and O'ne before."

"I know Al. Now get out of here."

༃ ༃ ༃

"...think about her. But I know that she has forgiven me and now I can forgive myself," Al disclosed.

Dead Roots Wilting Flower

"Where were you? I thought I lost you," Dr. King questioned.

"I don't understand."

"Never mind. I think that we can cut our sessions back to an 'as needed' basis. What do you think?"

"That sounds good to me, Dr. King," Al replied, nodding his head in agreement.

Chapter 18

As Len slowly fell out of a deep sleep, his mind was filled with questions, questions that required answers before he could get out of bed. Over and over again, his mind reviewed and played back into his lost short-term memory, yesterday's late-night activities. Slowly, some of the details outlining the who, what, when, and how of this woman's presence were being filled in.

"Who's body is that over there? For that matter, where in the hell am I?" Len shouted within his head, straining to remember.

He breathed a sigh of relief as the remembrance of a name settled into his head. It was all coming back to him.

She wasn't much to look at. Hell, she's not even five-feet tall and most likely in her late twenties. With his eyes closed, he was still able to see her short red hair and a pair of hollow, oversized dark brown eyes that possessed no sparkle.

Their conversation at the dinner dance, which was being hosted by the local chapter of 100 Black Men, was laid back and full of fun. Their introduction to one another was facilitated by being seated side by side while having dinner at the function. They both were beyond the normal phony norm of people that generally attended this type of event. Thus, Len was very surprised when she formed her mouth into a mannish smile and asked him to take her home.

"I don't want to drive after drinking. Which way are you headed when you leave here?" she inquired of Len, who also had consumed his fair share of drinks.

Len was equally surprised at the words that came out of his mouth since he wasn't remotely attracted to this woman.

"I'm going north but just let me know when you're ready to leave and I'll take you wherever you want to go," Len offered with a smile.

"Why don't we stay a minute or two longer then and have another drink?" She suggested, knowing what she wanted would be easier to get after a few more drinks.

Minutes turned into almost two hours. The time was spent in light conversation and they both lost track of how many drinks they each consumed. The crowd inside the bar area of the Michigan Avenue Hilton ballroom was so heavy that their departure went without notice.

The amount that both of them had drank mandated that neither of them drive. A slow cab ride, under the curious eye of the driver, facilitated an exchange of heavy kissing and feeling of each other's bodies. The cab ride confirmed each of their expectations.

The transition from the cab into her Lincoln Park brownstone apartment was done fluidly so as not to ruin the momentum. No awkward moments of indecisiveness occurred.

They both wanted the same thing, so it came as no surprise that once in the house that she removed her blouse to reveal two thumbnail-sized nipples that were accompanied by an almost nonexistent cleavage. Len pulled her close and hoisted her small frame up into his arms. She immediately wrapped her legs around his waist and leaned back to admire what she had caught.

Her dark nipples in sight and within range, Len couldn't resist the temptation and brushed the edge of his little finger's nail against her left breast. She reacted as if someone had just touched an electric wire to her body. Len mistook her reaction as something special that he had done. In fact, she needed and wanted what he had to offer from the waist down. To this end, her breasts were extremely sensitive when she was about to get what she needed.

In bed first, she wrapped herself tightly inside of the bed covers and affected a passive demeanor. She knew that she didn't have to be aggressive to get what she wanted. What she wanted was at the side of the bed quickly removing his clothes.

Len stripped down to a blood-red Joe Boxer thong and stepped over to the bed so that she could admire what he was offering. With his neatly trimmed hair allowing the thong to do its job, he received the reaction that he wanted as she started looking him up and down with approving eyes. Len looked back with a yearning look that said a wordless, "Can I join you?"

She was too busy admiring Len's well-defined chest and six-pack stomach to notice Len's longing.

"I'm standing here naked, cold and with a major hard-on calling your name, Myra," Len informed her in a sexy voice that only, someone with his experience could command.

"Myra! Yes, that's your name," popped into Len's mind as he thought back.

With a slight grin in a very low and husky voice, Myra suggested, "Why don't you join me in here?"
Time being of the essence, she made her point clear by holding the bed's sheer golden-rod-colored spread open in an inviting manner. Entering, Len knew what he wanted but had no idea what he was in for.
Knowing how sensitive her nipples were, Len began kissing, licking, nibbling, and kneading with his lips her fully erect nipples, all in a soft way. By the time that he worked his way from the left side to the right, she was telling him, in a voice should have come from someone much bigger, "Get it baby. Get it baby."
She said it over and over until Len wanted to get all of it. In his mind, at the moment, there was not a more substantial chest in the world. He was getting it because she was giving it. Wanting to see what else there was, he slowly worked his way down her flat stomach and paused just above her hair.
Old habits being hard to break, he paused for just a second to sniff the air for odors emanating from their heavy petting. None being detected, Len gently worked his middle finger into her softness while gently and expertly licking the outermost edges of her pussy until it started twitching in anticipation of his mouth and finger's next movements.
Removing his middle finger from its job, Len placed it in his mouth and sucked her from it.
"You're so sweet," Len said, savoring her smell, her taste, and the shocked look on her face.

"You need to take it easy with me. OK? It's been a long time since I've had a man," she informed Len.

"I understand," Len replied thinking that his experience allowed him to know exactly what she meant.

He positioned himself beside her and began giving tender kisses everywhere.

Myra, having not been with a man for over a year, was surprised at how good her choice was. His attentive way was just what she was looking for. It was those slam-bam-thank-you-mam encounters that had turned her from men to women a few years back. Now, every now and then she wanted to be with a man just to hit that certain spot and erase a craving that only a real man with a real dick could do for her.

Once convinced that this was really what she wanted, Myra took control of the love-making. She knew what she wanted and she only had this one night to get it. She wanted a quick one first. Using all the leverage that her small frame could muster, with her hands on the headboard — she had loosened up nicely — she rode him fiercely. It was still snug, but she was accommodating his beige-colored dick just fine.

Feeling that his ejaculation was imminent, she rose up off of him to a popping sound followed by the hissing of air escaping from her. She rose off of him wanting to be sure that if he were a one-hit wonder, she at least would get hers.

The feeling and sound of her unplugging from him was enough to push her over the top. When she popped off of him, her juices started flowing down the length of his shaft.

Having her needs only partially met, she wanted to get things started again quickly. Wasting no more time worrying whether or not he could get the job done, she reached down and put him back into her where she needed him.

She was up and down and back and forth at the same time with a feverish quickness. It didn't take long. She slowed down the pace when she felt his body tensing. Moments later she felt him explode repeatedly inside of her. His juice hit her insides like a sharp whip snapping this way and that way, extending her pleasure. Now it was time for the good part.

Myra wanted to curl his toes. She wanted him to think back on this night and never forget that he was with the best he ever had. She slid off of him and kneeled between his legs admiring her work. He looked spent. She bent over and engulfed his soft dick in her mouth.

Just as he was beginning to harden, she took her mouth off of him and used her tongue to lick the base of his balls all the way up to the tip of his now fully erect rod, forcing the saliva from her tongue and letting it coat every inch of him. Once he was licked to her satisfaction, she blew gentle breezes over his cooling, erect cock, her breath causing the skin in the area to crawl.

Len lay on his back, with his eyes closed, moaning from being teased in a new way. With the moan and his skin's reaction, Myra knew that she had him, and she decided to be selfish and offer him nothing else but pussy for as long as he could stand it. She would not give him any more mouth, definitely no ass, and she was finished kissing this man. She just wanted to fuck his brains out and move on.

"Shit, this is about me," Myra acknowledged to herself.

Somewhere around five in the morning sleep overcame them: Myra, from sheer exhaustion and Len since he wasn't being kept up anymore.

ℑ ℑ ℑ

Dead Roots Wilting Flower

    Remembering now, Len started to contemplate his escape. He wanted to be his usual self and get out with little or no fuss. Lying here, he contemplated three options while he relaxed enough to start enjoying the physical release that his body was still experiencing.
    Option one was a quick getaway. He could jump up and start dressing while vividly explaining how late he was for an early appointment. Option two entailed a little small talk, an exchange of phone numbers, and a few promises. Promises that most likely would never be kept. Option three was for him to roll over right now and try to rekindle what had been there during the night before.
    Len allowed himself to visualize what he enjoyed most about the night. This woman had held him in her hands, between her fingers, and licked and loved its entire length as if he were the proud owner of the last dick on earth. There was something about what she did that made him want to do it again.
    There was nothing new about the physical sensations that he felt — he had felt them all before — but the aura that overcame him stemmed from how she held it, how she loved it, how she honored it with her all — that was new to him. Any man would want to feel that again, Len reassured himself as he continued to fantasize to himself while he lay there.
    Wimping out, he chose option two, mostly since he hated rejection more then he loved sex. Mustering up the mental fortitude to face the task at hand, he turned his body to face her. He didn't expect to meet her eyes — eyes that were wide open as if they had been reading his thoughts through the back of his head. Hollow eyes that were covering her thoughts. Thoughts that were very similar to Len's.
    "Good morning," Len greeted her.
    "Good morning. I'm surprised that you're still here."

"Well, I was thinking — you know, just thinking that I wasn't ready to leave and face not ever seeing you again. I mean, uh, is that possible?" Len questioned her and himself at the same time.

"Be careful, boy, you might just get what you ask for. You don't even know me and you want to see me again?"

"No, I was just thinking. Is there anything wrong with that?"

"Len, I'm seeing someone. My girlfriend lets me step out from time to time to experience how the other side does it. There's no mistake about it, I'm hers," Len was informed.

"Oh, I see," Len said in a rejected voice.

"Don't sound like that. You're good. Really good. The best man I've ever had."

The smile on her face showed that she meant what she said.

"You're still not a girl," Myra asserted to keep his mind clear.

"What does that mean?"

"It's just different that's all. After today maybe I'll introduce you to my other half and we can all do this again. Anyway, why don't we get cleaned up and then I can treat you to some breakfast at the Y," she offered, rubbing her inner thigh to make her point clear.

Looking at Len's reaction, her power amazed her.

꒒ ꒒ ꒒

Len made it home at seven that evening and, like clockwork, as he had for months he felt the need to call Kayla. It wasn't sex — he couldn't have sex again if his life depended on it. His desire for Kayla was stronger than sex.

The phone rang fifteen times.

Dead Roots Wilting Flower

"No answer; no answer; no answer," Len screamed, banging the phone down onto its cradle and watching it fall to the floor.

Len's mind knew that all of this was Al's fault. There is an unspoken code among friends that friends don't entertain their friend's girl under any circumstances. "Ex" or not. The only remaining issue in his mind was what he was going to do about it. Right now, anything was possible.

Len picked up the phone from the floor and dialed Al's number.

"... Al this is Len ... I've been trying to get in contact with Kayla. Have you seen her? ... How in the world are you going to tell me that its not a good time for me to talk to her ... Listen, Al, just be straight-up with me. Are you seeing her? ... Don't give me that bull shit double talk. I asked you a simple question. Are you seeing Kayla? ... Yeah, right. I thought we were boys. How can you make a move on my girl? ... That's because there is nothing you can say. You're just a back-stabbing low-life snake-in-the-grass asshole ... Don't let me catch you because I'm going to put my foot so far up your ass that you're gonna taste shoe leather ... Yeah, yeah, whatever. Like I said, your ass is mine when I see you."

Len slammed the phone down in Al's ear.
"Who in the hell does he think he is? It's on," Len screamed into the air. "His ass is mine."

Chapter 19

Tracie was feeling the effects of being up half the night thinking about what she was going to say to Al. The lack of sleep was not wearing well on her already worn face. What she was contemplating wasn't any of her business at all, but she felt she had to get involved for Al's sake as well as her own.

The proposition of betrayal was not enough to keep her up the entire night. What was troubling her was how she would bring up someone's secret and not seem to be betraying the confidence of a friend. At the end of the night she decided that she wanted what she wanted so the end justified the means.

Wanting to show her best side, Tracie opted against her normal boring work attire. Just to be on the safe side, she wore a low-cut, tight-fitting, cream-colored mohair sweater that was cropped just above her waist. She complemented her sweater with a pair of tight-fitting, black-hip hugger designer jeans.

As soon as she arrived at work, she went on the prowl for Al and found him checking the routing slips on a couple of oversized boxes.

"Hey, Al. How did things go in court?" Tracie cheerfully asked.

The question really didn't have to be asked. Tracie knew that if things had have gone well, Al would have filled his work station with excitement. That's the kind of guy he was. His true feelings and emotions always showed, revealing his mood like words clearly printed in bold letters on an otherwise blank sheet of paper.

"Just more of the same," Al replied to Tracie's inquiry.

Looking up at her, he noticed the drawn look under her eyes and asked, "Who whipped you? It looks like Ali punched you in both of your eyes."

"No, they just get puffy and dark when I haven't slept. I was up all night thinking."

There was a period of silence. Al knew Tracie was going to tell him what she had been up all night thinking about.

"What are you doing for lunch today? Do you want to go and get something to eat?"

"I don't have any plans yet. Why not? I see that you're dressed for it. Are you sure that you want to be seen with someone like me as nicely dressed as you are?"

"Do you like?" Tracie asked and gave a model's spin. She was happy that he had noticed her.

"You know you have a slamming body, and with that gear, you're going to tease men all afternoon. Whose attention are you trying to get?"

"You know I only have eyes for you," Tracie said in a flirtatious voice.

"Yeah, right. Where do you want to go for lunch?"

"How about getting some Harold's?"

"That sounds good. I'll find you about five and we will go."

Tracie settled into Al's car and let her mind roam. She did like riding with him. He handled a car as skillfully as he handled her the two times that she was lucky enough to talk herself up on some of him.

Continuing her mental ramble, she took a few seconds to linger on the memory of the warm feeling that accompanied a full body massage that Al had provided on one of their nights together. She could almost feel the way he had worked his strong hands over her body, made her purr, and forced her to relax.

As Al turned the car onto Canal Street, Tracie remained in her mental state of ramble. In her mind, she was in the bedroom with him in a state of arousal. He was the only man she had ever been with that made her feel that spending time together was more important than having sex. She was hot and bothered and he didn't even care. Not able to take much more, she had had no choice but to demand what she wanted, Tracie remembered.

Kissing, licking, and sucking his indifference away, it wasn't long before I had what I wanted. He wasn't easy. He made me work for it. Once I got it, he wasn't selfish with it. Once he started giving it, my body started telling him that he could have me. As much as he wanted.

The motion of Al turning the car sharply snapped Tracie from the past to the present.

"Nope, a passive lover isn't going to get satisfied. I'll be dammed if I'm going to be passive now," Tracie reflected.

In Harold's they both ordered five wings and drinks. Al ordered his with salt, pepper, hot sauce, and mild sauce and Tracie with just salt and pepper. After getting their orders, they settled into a booth and dug into their meals.

"You know, sitting here I just can't get over how much I really care about you," Tracie stated, forgetting to swallow the chicken that was in her mouth before she spoke.

Wondering where her comment was leading, Al was hesitant to reply. In an effort to buy himself a little time to assess Tracie's motives, he took his time chewing the food that was in his mouth and followed swallowing it with a long draw of his twenty-four ounce Mountain Dew through a straw. Still not ready to reply, he began to speak not knowing what to say.

"Girl, you know that you're my homey. Work wouldn't be the same without you there."

"It's more than that, Al. When something is going on with you I want to know about it and be part of it. If there's something you need to know, then I should tell you, right?" Tracie asked.

"I would hope so. So who's been talking shit at work now?"

"This isn't really about work. You're probably going to kill me for being in your business."

"Friends can talk about anything," Al assured her.

"You know that Kayla and I talk, right?" Tracie questioned.

"No, I didn't," Al replied in a perturbed voice. "You know the last time I checked, her business was her business. So maybe we all should mind our own business."

Al's tone was serious.

"Well, I don't think you should see her anymore. Besides, if you need something, I'm always here for you."

Dead Roots Wilting Flower

"Tracie, you can't be all up in my personal business like that."

"I'm just trying to tell you that I care about you. Tell you that I want . . ."

Tracie paused, rethinking what she was about to say. Her thoughts together, she began again.

"I want the best for you. Maybe there are some things that you don't know about her. Things that could hurt you."

"You're crazy. Let's get out of here. I have a load to deliver and I don't have time for this."

Losing her composure, she inquired, "Why can't you see that I'd do anything for you? You want to chase after that piece of woman who's pregnant with a gay man's child? Who just had to go and get an AIDS test instead of being with me?"

Tracie was giving off much attitude.

The word AIDS stood out and rung loudly in Al's head. The words were ringing so loudly that he thought he was losing his mind. The only thing that was clear to him was that he had to get away from Tracie.

"Tracie, that's none of my business, and I don't want to know that kind of stuff from you about someone else. What kind of friend do you call yourself? You can't go around telling people's business."

"You know you have to be careful and look out for things like that. I didn't tell her to go out and get AIDS."

"You don't just go out and betray a confidence like that. Not only have you betrayed her but you have hurt our friendship too."

"OK, I'm guilty. If I'm wrong for caring and wanting to be with you, then I'm wrong. I just can't stop how I feel about you."

"Look, we're co-workers and friends — that's it — nothing more. I'm ready to go," Al stated, feeling that he had to find Kayla as soon as possible!

☪ ☪ ☪

"Al, what are you doing here?" Kayla asked in a voice level that could only be heard by Al and not the other late night office workers who might be straining to hear their conversation.

Directing him to an empty conference room just off of the reception area, Kayla couldn't keep from smiling on the inside at how he surprised her at work.

"OK Al, what's up! Why are you here?"

"Well, I was at work and I just couldn't stop thinking about you. You know, that can be dangerous," Al joked.

Not getting the smile that he wanted from Kayla, he continued. " I asked another driver to make my last run and here I am."

Kayla, shielding her feelings, responded, "Haven't you heard of a phone?"

The words were said with a look of mock disgust on her face and in her persona.

"You know, sometimes the phone just won't do," Al smiled and spoke at the same time.

Moving closer to where she was standing, Al reached for and took hold of both of her hands and gave them a reassuring squeeze in an effort to calm her. Looking deeply at her, he quietly said with force, in a voice no louder than a whisper, "I love you."

"Have you lost your mind?" Kayla replied.

Trembling on the inside, Kayla thoughtfully continued. "You have no idea what you're saying."

There was a look of extreme concern on her face.

The expression on Al's face didn't change. He was ready for anything. His words didn't change either. Self-

Dead Roots Wilting Flower

assuredly, he repeated, "I love you" and moved closer into her personal space, waiting for her reply.

Her resolve softening, she held her breath for a second. Wanting what she knew she had no right to want, she didn't give in when she willed herself to offer, "Look, Al, I have issues."

"I love you," Al reaffirmed like a knight ready to do battle for what he wanted.

This time he was determined not to take a fall from grace as he had done in the past. His face was so close to Kayla's that she could actually taste the sweetness of his breath as his fast-paced breathing flowed in and out from between his lips.

It was a taste that engulfed her and was calming at the same time. He just tasted and felt right. Standing here, savoring a man laying it all on the line just for her, her eyes rolled into the back of her head and she came. Her physical reaction was the byproduct of finally being loved by someone whom she knew she could really love back.

Again, making his point ever so clear, Al repeated, "I love you."

He was so close now that when the last word glided out of his mouth, his lips slightly brushed against hers and she felt his love. His love started at her lips, skipped her brain, and went straight to her heart, which was caught by surprise. It wasn't ready for this. In an effort to brace itself, her heart skipped a beat.

Her mind had not caught up with her heart, but she began to speak anyway.

"Al, I love you too, but..."

Stopped in mid-sentence, Al's lips didn't let anything else escape from her mouth. The kiss was good and took her words and fears away.

When the kiss was over, he read her eyes and replied, "I know. And whatever the issue is, it doesn't change the fact that I still love you."

Eyes filled with tears and face filled with emotion, Kayla withdrew from his embrace. "You don't know. I'm not fit to love. I might have..."

Al cut her off again this time revealing a knightly sword.

"How can you question what God has put on our hearts? You're not the only one who has problems. We'll see them through. Just don't turn your back on love."

Having nowhere else to go, Kayla fell into his arms and cried uncontrollably.

Chapter 20

Four days. The days had come and gone. It was ever so clear to James that Kayla had made up her mind that she was not going to see him again while he was in Chicago. His priorities needed to change. The days that he called off work to stay in Chicago had not paid off. His mind made-up, he was going back to New York.

Thinking back about what happened, he was hard pressed to blame her for not returning any of his calls over the last few days. He knew that it was asking her to accept a lot. Still, in the back of his mind he felt that if she truly loved him, she would be able to accept his past.

His heart told him that he still loved her. But mind reminded him that over the last two weeks he had unsuccessfully tried to move hell and high water to win her back. He decided it was time to go. It was time to move on from a woman who did not want him any more.

James was startled from his thoughts by a hard knock on the room's door. He assumed it was the maid trying to get a head start on cleaning the room he was about to vacate.

"Just a second," James called out toward the room door.

Moving toward the door, he decided to kill two birds with one stone and picked up his suitcase before opening it.

"Mr. Anderson?" A strange white man confronted James when he opened the door.

"Yes, I am Mr. Anderson. Can I help you?"

"Mr. Anderson, my name is Maurice Short. I am an investigator from the Chicago Board of Health," the man stated and then paused for a second or two to let his presence sink in and to assess his contact's reaction, just as his training had taught him to do.

"Mr. Anderson, your name was given to us as a sexual contact of someone who was recently tested for the Human Immune Deficiency Virus by our office."

James immediately knew that Richard the waiter boy must have given his name and room number to these people.

"No, Mr. Short, I don't think I have a problem. I think that it's just someone trying to get back at me. I haven't been exposed to AIDS. Now if you don't mind, I have a plane to catch."

James was firm with the man, leaving no doubt that he was finished with this conversation.

Mr. Short, noticing James' demeanor, went into a well-rehearsed spiel.

"We can't make you come in to be tested Mr. Anderson, but we do want you to know that there is a fairly good chance that you have been exposed to the

Dead Roots Wilting Flower

virus. This is real and not a joke. The prudent thing to do is to get tested to protect yourself and the ones you love."

"OK. I hear you loud and clear, but I don't have time for this right now. I have a plane to catch," James responded, trying to placate the insistent figure in front of him.

Mr. Short reached into his bag and pulled out three brightly colored papers and handed them to James.

"I brought some brochures that you can review."

"I'll read them later but right now I have to go," James insisted.

Closing the door, James' mind drifted back to when he had lodged his complaint with the hotel against Richard. He wanted to make sure that the vindictive waiter would not be serving drinks and hitting on hotel patrons anymore. Now, after this visit by the Board of Health, he wished he would have taken a more personal approach, found Richard and kicked his ass.

Ready to leave the room with his bags, James was still bothered by having been reported to the Board of Health. He contemplated taking another day in Chicago to find Richard and teach him a lesson he would never forget. Seconds went by and, with the passage of time, his fury began to dissipate.

Knowing he was out of time, he let the thought of taking his frustrations out on Richard slip from his mind and decided to go home. It was clear to him that he had had enough of Chicago and was ready to get out of Dodge. He hadn't accomplished what he came for. James wasn't used to not getting what he wanted, and the loss of Kayla wasn't sitting well with him. Getting back to New York was the best thing for him and his piece of mind.

Chapter 21

Kayla was nervous about going for her test results. Riding in a Checker cab, she was beginning to second-guess her decision to get the results alone. The cab made a left turn onto 39th Street, less then a block away from the building, and she was still barely able to control her emotions.

Breathing deep, hard breaths, she was able to get her nerves in order as the cab started to slow. Getting out of the cab in front of the building, she handed the driver a ten-dollar bill to pay for her six-dollar fare and told the driver to keep the change.

"Can you come back and get me in about an hour?" Kayla asked the driver.

"Sure I can. Take my card. It has my cell number on it. Call me when you're ready and I'll come back and fetch you," the driver assured her. He was hungry for the fare.

"Thank you," Kayla said through a forced smile, trying to show her gratitude to the cab driver.

"About how long do you think you will be?" the driver asked in hastened English that had been practiced since arriving to Chicago from South Africa.

"I really don't know but I would guess less than two hours."

"Just call me, OK?" The driver looked directly into Kayla's eyes to judge the sincerity of her promise to call him.

"I will. Thank you."

Walking through the building's door, she knew she was ready. Maybe the time she was spending with Dr. King was helping. She was firmly into the present.

"Number 57896A," a husky female voice called into a waiting room where seven women sat anxiously.

"That's me," Kayla replied and rose from her chair, letting the "Good Housekeeping" magazine that she had been reading fall from her lap onto the floor.

Not bothering to pick up the magazine, Kayla's eyes were fixated on the husky woman's face. She was about fifty, Kayla noted, as she searched for her eyes.

The older woman protected her eyes like a jury foreman about to read a guilty verdict. Kayla continued her search and was momentarily successful. As quickly as she made contact the woman directed her eyes to the ground, not wanting to look directly at Kayla.

"Oh no," Kayla softly exclaimed.

"What's wrong?" The woman asked in a calm voice.

"Nothing," Kayla lied.

Kayla knew the results. She read the woman like a book. The rest of her time at the building was a blur to her. All she wanted was to get the hell out of there.

Dead Roots Wilting Flower

Knowing what she knew and knowing herself, she wasn't sure know how much longer she could keep it together.

Kayla was not interpreting any of the words that seemed to just keep flowing from the husky woman's mouth. Feeling as if the walls of the building were moving in on her, her emotions told her that she had to get out of there. Not acting on her feeling, she remained seated in the husky woman's office. Forcing herself, somehow Kayla was able to force words out of her mouth: "I have to go. Can I come back on another day?"

"OK. That's fine. What about coming back tomorrow?" the woman asked, not wanting a client who needed help to fall through the cracks.

Surprised that she was still sitting in the office, Kayla strained and made her voice respond. "I don't know. I will call and set a time."

Finally outside of the building, she was desperately trying to hold it together. On her cell phone, Kayla dialed the number on the cab driver's card.

"I'm sorry, Ms., I didn't know you were going to need a ride so soon. You told me it was going to be a couple of hours. I'm all the way at O'Hare Airport, and with traffic the way it is, it would be at least an hour before I could get to you," the driver said in an apologetic voice.

"OK. OK. I understand. Thanks anyway."

It was just how her luck was going. Needing what she needed, Kayla dialed Al's cell number and was calmed slightly when his voice brushed against and caressed her ear when he answered the phone. He spoke a throaty hello.

"... Can you come and get me? ... I'm at the Board of Health on 39th ... Please, Al, don't ask. Can we talk when you get here? ... Please hurry. I'm about to die in this place ... Ten minutes is fine. I'll be out in front of the building ... Thank you. I'll see you when you get here."

Al pulled up to the front of the building with reckless abandon after spotting Kayla sitting on the front stairs with her head in her hands. Not caring how he parked, the passenger side tires of his car were a good two feet onto the sidewalk next to the building.

Out of the car in a flash, Al rushed to Kayla's side. She was rocking from side to side and not responding to him when he called her name. He knew that she was somewhere else.

"Woman, don't do this to me! Come on, help me," Al implored, shaking Kayla's limp body back and forth.

With Kayla not responding, Al's actions were beginning to draw looks from people going in and out of the Board of Health building. He needed to do something.

Taking matters into his own hands, Al reached out and gathered Kayla into his arms. A man in control, to him she felt like she weighed nothing in his arms. His love was all the strength he needed. In seconds she was lying across the back seat of his car, and he was behind the wheel on his way to his house.

♫ ♫ ♫

"Come sit with me, baby girl."

Being called "baby girl" brought earlier visits to her memory. When she was a little girl, before her fear forced her to shut him out, he would affectionately call her his baby girl. He was there now, and for the first time she knew who he was. It was the first time in all of her years that she freely and completely let a vision enter her mind. As the vision moved through her, events went very fast. Surprisingly, the speed didn't impact the crystal clarity of her vision.

Dead Roots Wilting Flower

"Grandpapa. It's been you all the time. Why have you been with me?"

"I needed you."

His voice sounded to her ears like he swallowed a very old man. An old man that had to be at least three times the age of the fortyish man who was within her mind. The voice stayed within her and comforted her in a way that was before unknown to her.

It was the voice of someone who would accept her just the way she was. Her Grandpapa had stood watch over her on many days biding his time waiting for his chance to be fully heard and understood.

The voice bespoke the unconditional love of a grandparent for his grandchild. The voice's vibrancy made it clear that she would no longer have to search for unconditional love again. Through her grandfather, John Lewis, it was hers to treasure forever.

"Baby girl, I need you to do something for me. You know that everything is going to be OK? Just take it one day at a time, baby girl. Someone is always there looking out for you."

"I'm in so much trouble, Grandpapa."

"Things are how they are supposed to be. All of your life you have been trying to be in control. You wanted to be in control so much that it has taken me all these years to get you to talk to me. I was beginning to think that you were never going to let me in."

His speech was interrupted by his drawn out laugh, which rumbled through Kayla.

"Baby girl, I want you to just relax and let God be in full control. He'll work everything out."

"I will, Grandpapa. I will."

"Now I need you to do something for me. Please pray for me. Pray and ask God to forgive me for the man I killed. You know from what I told you over the years that

I've made some mistakes. I need prayer from your side. I can't do it from here."

Very few words were needed for her to understand what he was saying to her. He had been with her for so long that Kayla knew his thoughts almost simultaneously as he was thinking them.

Kayla slowly came out of her trance-like state. As she came out, she recalled many of the memories she had over the years. It all came together. Her roots began to take hold, and she felt strong. Strong enough to endure and see a future.

Kayla unwillingly began to come to while holding tightly to the coolness of a pillow that smelled lightly of Burberry cologne. Feeling comfortable, she lingered right where she was, in a space where she felt that everything was right. A space where you can't stay for long, but while you're there it's like magic.

Venturing out of her comfort zone, Kayla opened her eyes but did not move. It was a man's room. She searched her mind and reasoned that it had to be Al's.

"Al, are you there?" Kayla called.

"I'll be right there," Al called from the kitchen into the bedroom where Kayla was.

A few seconds later, Al appeared in the doorway.

"So you're among the living, huh."

"I guess so. Thanks for coming to get me."

"Why did you try to go there by yourself?"

"I thought the news would be good and that would be that. Why worry people needlessly?"

"Yeah, but you have to pray for the best and prepare for the worst."

"I know. Anyway, it's good that I went. Some things have come to me, and I've made up my mind about a few things."

"There's plenty of time for that. You've been out for hours. Are you hungry? I made some spaghetti and garlic bread."

"That sounds good. Just give me a second to get myself together."

"No, you just sit tight. I'll get everything you need. I laid out one of my shirts for you to slip into so you can be comfortable."

Al waited for a response from her. When she didn't respond he continued.

"Don't worry, I won't try to see if you have on pink panties under the shirt."

Al was all smiles as he walked from the room while Kayla lay back and let the comfort of Al's bed engulf her in a way that only happens in a bed that belongs to a couple.

Chapter 22

"...Hello, mama. How are you? ... I'm OK. I have some things that I have to talk to you about. Are you sitting down? ... I had to give up the baby ... It has nothing to do with James. I found out that I am HIV positive ... No. I wouldn't bring a baby into this. It wouldn't be fair ... Well God is going to have to forgive me. I had to do what He put on my heart ... See, mama that's what I mean. I should have never told you. You can't run my life ... No, mama I'm not coming home ... No, I don't want you to come here either. I have some real soul searching to do over the next few days ... No, mama. I have so much on my mind. I just want some time alone to think ... It's too late for me to second-guess that. I did what I thought was right for the baby and for me ... I'm going to go now, mama ... I love you too and I know that you're there for me ... I will ... OK ... Tell everybody I said hi ... Oh, by the way, don't you go calling James

Anderson telling him any of my business ... Do I have your word? ... Thank you, mama. I'll call you in a few days."

Kayla knew that she couldn't take the chance that her mother might call James. She decided to be a woman about it and do the right thing and call him. Not waiting to lose her nerve, Kayla dialed James' New York number and listened to the phone ringing, thinking about how much she had changed in the last month since she had last seen him.

"... James ... I know that I should have called you sooner but I just didn't have it in me to face you after that scene in the hotel room ... Slow down. I have some things that you need to know before you say anything about that day ... James, just stop. There are some things that are bigger than that ... James, I was pregnant with your child ... No, I'm not still pregnant. I had to have an abortion ... You're not listening to me. I had to have an abortion. I am HIV positive ... I don't think I gave *you* anything. You need to check your lifestyle before you start pointing fingers ... Why don't we have this conversation some other time? You are rubbing me the wrong way ... I didn't do anything but try to love you. You're the one who messed us up and now most likely you have ruined the rest of both of our lives ... Just check yourself and don't do this to anybody else ... I don't want to hear it, James. I have to go. Bye."

Kayla hung up the phone in James' ear. She was proud of herself. She had faced James, even if it was over the phone, told him what she had to tell him, and held herself together while doing it. She had no idea what she was going to do next, but it felt as if a thousand-pound weight had been lifted from her heart. Now her mind raced to Al. She wondered how court was going for him.

☽ ☽ ☽

Court was not due to convene for the afternoon session for another five or six minutes. Attorney Holt decided to use the waiting time wisely. She slowly walked over to the judge's clerk, contemplating what she was going to say.

"Hey, Attorney Holt, how are you? Look, I have some new pictures of my baby." The clerk eagerly pushed the snapshots to the attorney and smiled a loving mother's smile.

"She is lovely. The pictures show so much of her personality," Attorney Holt replied, still studying the photographs.

"She is so amazing. Every day she learns something new and surprises me with it," the clerk proudly uttered.

"Children are astonishing, aren't they?" Attorney Holt replied, and handed the frame full of photos back to the clerk.

"Thanks for the picture frame. Everybody loves it."

"You're more than welcome. What number is the Gold case on the list?" Attorney Holt inquired.

"You're third on the list."

"Third! I'm on pins and needles. I wanted to be first," Attorney Holt responded, using her best acting ability.

"You guys don't have anything to worry about," the clerk said with a smile and affirming nod of her head.

"Thanks. I'm going to read over my notes to make sure I'm ready. Kiss your baby for me OK?"

The clerk nodded her head and took on a more formal demeanor, hearing the judge entering the courtroom.

Attorney Holt was pleased with the results of her twenty-five-dollar frame investment. Sure it was nice to do something good for the young mother, but it was just as important to have the clerk feel comfortable enough with her to let her know that the custody hearing was going well.

In light of the clerk's encouraging remarks, Attorney Holt planned to be less aggressive in front of Judge Nixon. There was no reason to risk changing the judge's opinion. She planned on just reacting to the arguments made in the courtroom.

The first two cases were called and disposed of in short order. It was clear that the judge was not in the best of moods. When the attorneys tried to make far-fetched arguments, she cut them off, not wanting to spend time listening to them. Before long the Gold case was called and they were in front of Judge Nixon.

Attorney Holt began.

"Your honor, this is in re the matter of O'ne Gold vs. Albert Gold. Mr. Gold's emergency motion for the immediate possession of his minor child was continued to today for a report from supportive services."

"Good afternoon, your honor. Bernie Leverwitz on behalf of the maternal grandparents, Mr. and Mrs. Clark."

"Birdie Mae Jordan from the Department of Children and Family Services."

"Your honor, we have done everything that was requested of us. Today we request that Mr. Gold's child, O'ne, be released from the custody of DCFS to him," Attorney Holt stated in a confident tone.

"I have reviewed the supportive services report, but before I rule I want to hear from Ms. Jordan and have her explain what DCFS is recommending," Judge Nixon said.

"Your honor, we have looked into the background of Mr. Gold and found no reason why he could not provide a safe and loving environment for the child. We also interviewed Mr. Gold's girlfriend who is an integral part of his life and believe that she would help with raising the

Dead Roots Wilting Flower

child. At this time we recommend that the child be placed in Mr. Gold's care."

"Your honor, I don't think that the Clarks should be just overlooked as suitable guardians of their granddaughter," Attorney Leverwitz pleaded.

Judge Nixon looked at Attorney Leverwitz with a stare of disbelief and began, "I find that the Clark's have placed the child in harm's way. I am not going to place the child back in that environment. What I can do for your clients is entertain a written motion for visitation by the grandparents. That is, if you decide to file one. Right now I am making a ruling based upon the facts that I have before me. I am going to grant Mr. Gold's motion. Please draw up an order, Ms. Holt."

Judge Nixon turned to her clerk and asked that the next case be called.

Al could hardly contain himself as he raced out of the courtroom to call Kayla and let her know the news.

"Kayla! We won! We won! ... Everything went perfectly ... I don't know but I'll find out. You know that I want it to be as soon as possible ... OK. I'll call you from the car ... Bye."

"There's that bastard," Mr. Clark mumbled to himself, walking toward Al.

"You think you won. That's OK. This is the white man's justice. You still have to face street justice," Mr. Clark cautioned Al.

"Hey, old man, there is no justice for someone who tries to take another man's child," Al hit back stingingly.

"You have stepped in some shit that you can't get off of you, boy. What you did to my daughter and now my family stinks and you are going to pay for it," Mr. Clark promised.

"Right now, just get the hell out of my face. I'm not going to tell you again," Al firmly forewarned.

With his last word said in such an ominous manner, Al began to back away. The intensity of the interaction between the two men was escalating, and the last thing that he needed after winning today was to let an old man thug bring him down to his level.

No matter how bad he wanted to continue the verbal attack, Al understood that nothing good could come from a fight in the courthouse. He had already won.

Attorney Holt, walking out of the courtroom just as Al was about to reenter it, gave Al a million-dollar smile as she approached him.

"Thank you, Attorney Holt. Thank you," Al repeated as the two of them took the elevator to the lobby of the courthouse.

"You know that good things happen to good people," the wise old attorney told Al.

"I know. I am going to do everything I can to make sure that O'ne has the best of everything."

"I know you will. I want you to meet me at my office in about an hour and we will go over how I want you to proceed with getting your daughter."

"OK. I'll see you then."

Chapter 23

The walk from Kayla's front porch to Al's car sat in the driveway was so familiar to him that he was walking on autopilot. During the seconds that it took for him to bounce down the front stairs, he was thought about how in just a few days everything in his life will have fallen into place.

After court and his meeting with Attorney Holt, Al enticed Kayla to take the afternoon off and spend it with him. They spent a light afternoon together, shopping for O'ne's arrival. A new bed, clothes, and toys were the major items purchased. At about seven that night they broke off their shopping expedition and went to visit O'ne at the foster home where she had been placed.

They spent a little over an hour visiting with O'ne and preparing her for the transition that was to take place at eleven the next morning. During the visit, they surprised O'ne with a new talking doll that said "daddy" among other things. Al was careful to watch for signs of O'ne being stressed. He saw none. Overall, Al thought that O'ne was in good sprits despite all that she had been through.

By the time Al's foot hit the concrete sidewalk at street level, his thoughts had turned to Kayla. Al knew that she was someone deserving of his love. He lingered on how effortlessly they were drawn to each other. After spending years working relationship after relationship trying to find the right one, the ease of true love was a breath of fresh air for him.

Al knew in his mind that once he became settled with O'ne he was going to ask Kayla to marry him. He was sure that with her illness, she would be a little hesitant at the thought of marriage. Al knew that with a lot of tender loving care, he could get her to overcome her fears. "Love is love and you have to take it when and how it comes. Nothing worth having is or stays perfect forever," Al thought.

Hitting the unlock button of the car's keyless entry system, Al began to focus on the task at hand. The air surrounding him seemed light. So light that he was startled by the voice that came out of nowhere behind him.

"Open all the doors and get in the damn car," a voice coolly but with authority called out from just behind him.

Al started to turn to see who was coming up behind him.

"There's no need for you to turn around. Just slide behind the wheel and start the car," the same voice directed.

Two men moved into the back seat of the car at the same time that Al slid into the driver's seat.

"Now look back here. I want you to see what you're up against," a man who had not spoken before told Al.

Dead Roots Wilting Flower

The cold metal of the sawed-off twelve-gauge shotgun that now rested firmly against his temple stopped the movement of Al's head. Out of the corner of his eye, he saw the dull metal of a Glock 40 being pointed between his eyes.

"Now we're going for a little ride," one of the men commanded.

By now it didn't matter which one of them was talking. Al knew them both and right now reviewing his options was the only thing on his mind. Unfortunately, not anticipating any problems, Al had left his gun at home. It was four against one, if you count the guns that the two men had, so Al decided to just play it cool.

The men directed Al to drive to Dan Ryan Woods on west 87th Street. Al knew that at this time of night there wouldn't be any help for him there. His best chance was going to be just as they were getting out of the car. After pulling into a parking space in the deserted forest preserve, Al turned the ignition off but didn't remove the keys.

"All right, we're going to get out of the car first, then you're going to follow us out. You got it?"

"Yeah. No problem," Al replied.

Knowing that this was his only chance, with the men halfway out of the car, Al reached to turn the ignition key and open the driver's door at the same time. He slammed the car into reverse and was able to throw both men out of the car.

To Al, it seemed as if it were taking forever for him to pick-up speed driving in reverse. He could hear the shotgun rounds pelting the metal on the front of the car.

Al's thoughts went from his own safety to, "Damn, now I'm going to need a new paint job."

Without any warning, caught by total surprise, the forty-caliber slug knocked the fire out of Al's chest. Instinctively, he stopped the car.

Al was taken by the fact that he couldn't will his body to move. Before too long it was as if he and his body were not one any more. At the same time as he felt his body leaving his control, Terow's words came to him in a loud voice.

"Until you get your life right, your roots are dead. You need these roots..."

It was too late.

Al's spirit watched as the ambulance pulled up and one of the two paramedics felt his neck for a pulse. He could hear them give up on him before they even started trying to revive him. He saw them take his body away. After they left, he went to comfort O'ne.

O'ne didn't understand his presence, she was too young. So he left and went back to Kayla's house.

Al was calm and gave Kayla directions for taking care of O'ne. Kayla didn't want to wake up from this vision. The vision was so very clear, and she didn't want it to be true.

"You know that you can't stay here with me for too long. Don't worry, you can go. I'll never truly leave you," Al assured her.

"Al, I love you. I'm going to stay here with you." Kayla spoke from her heart.

"I want you here with me but only when it's time. We have time," Al assured her. "You better go back now."

Chapter 24

Al's will requested that no funeral or fanfare be conducted because of his death. A simple memorial service at Brookin's Funeral Home and for his ashes to be spread over Lake Michigan was all that he asked for.

As the service moved on past the one-minute celebration of Al's life, Kayla was surprised that Len did not speak. The rest of the Las Vegas gang spoke at length. Tracie gave a heart-felt speech, telling what Al had brought to her life. Her talk ended when she broke down crying.

O'ne slowly walked toward Kayla, as she left the Dias, and with all the love that her two-year-old heart could muster, held her arms open. Her father's two true loves embraced each other for comfort.

Few made the trip to Lake Michigan to witness Al's final request. After the ashes were spread and the final words were spoken, Len made it a point to go over and comfort Tracie. He just had to have something that was Al's.

End Notes

O'ne, in all of her life, had never read anything as crystal clear and easy to understand as the manuscript in front of her. As she read, the words flowed, embraced her, and revealed the past while explaining many of the things she currently felt.

Turning the last page of the manuscript, O'ne looked at Attorney Holt. The older woman seemed to be somewhere else, enjoying the moment. Reflecting, O'ne understood where the woman was. For her, many of the blank spaces that existed before were now filled in.

O'ne, for the first time in her life, felt open. She knew that she had been loved unconditionally by those that mattered in her past. The feeling was settling to her. She felt that her roots were alive and expanding. Her roots would now be able to draw from the spirit all that she needed. She also understood that it was time to devote a part of her life to fulfilling her spiritual needs. If she were lucky, there would still be a few angels looking out for her.

"O'ne, thank you for sharing your trust with me. My heart is much lighter knowing for sure that it was their spirits helping me to hold on," Attorney Holt said after she came back to the present.

"Thanks for bringing the manuscript to me and for staying with me while I read it."

"You're welcome. I'm tired, baby. I think I will go on home."

O'ne watched the before-today unknown woman slowly walk toward her car, knowing that she would never see her again. Attorney Holt's work here was done. O'ne retired to her bedroom, and her prayers, to begin her own.

The End